NURSE IN THE SUN

Further Titles by Claire Rayner from Severn House

CHILDREN'S WARD
COTTAGE HOSPITAL
THE DOCTORS OF DOWNLANDS
THE FINAL YEAR
THE LONELY ONE
NURSE IN THE SUN
THE PRIVATE WING

NURSE IN
THE SUN

Claire Rayner

This revised edition complete with new introduction,
first published in Great Britain 1994 by
SEVERN HOUSE PUBLISHERS LTD of
9–15 High Street, Sutton, Surrey SM1 1DF.
Originally published in 1972 in paperback format only
under the pseudonym of Sheila Brandon.
First published in the USA 1994 by
SEVERN HOUSE PUBLISHERS INC., of
425 Park Avenue, New York, NY 10022.

British Library Cataloguing in Publication Data
Rayner, Claire
  Nurse in the Sun
  I. Title
  823.914 [F]

  ISBN 0-7278-4648-5

Typeset by Hewer Text Composition Services, Edinburgh.
Printed and bound in Great Britain by
Redwood Books, Trowbridge, Wiltshire.

Love is
a time of enchantment:
in it all days are fair and all fields
green. Youth is blest by it,
old age made benign: the eyes of love see
roses blooming in December,
and sunshine through rain. Verily
is the time of true-love
a time of enchantment – and
Oh! how eager is woman
to be bewitched!

The plane banked steeply, so that the wing rose high on one side to cut the sky with a sharp silvery line, and the fear that had thickened her throat when they took off but which had momentarily settled came bubbling up again. She turned her head to look out of the window beside her, but that was worse, for there below her – so very far below! – was a lurching patchwork of brownish green fields, the cluster of glass-gleaming black and red roofed buildings that was Gatwick airport, the crawling ants of cars on the grey ribbons of road, and this time she closed her eyes, and let her hands convulsively grip the buckle of her safety belt.

"There's no need to worry, you know," a deep voice murmured in her left ear. "Like, it's not going to fall out of the sky, or anything like that. We're turning south, that's all – on account of that's where we have to go, and the pilot had to use a cross runway because of the wind. But he'll start his real climb in a moment or so, and then we'll be right up over the clouds there and you won't be one bit scared. In fact, you feel better already, don't you?"

She had snapped her eyes open the moment he began to speak, staring at him. A wide face with a very square jaw, heavily freckled across the cheeks, brightly blue eyes under close-cut fair hair. Very American, she thought briefly, even before her mind registered the soft accent.

1

"I beg your pardon?" she said, and knew her voice sounded stiff and unfriendly.

"Well, now, there's no need to be ashamed of it! Tell you the truth, I reckon everybody, but *everybody* is scared of planes. Trouble is hardly anyone ever has the nerve to admit it. Now, me, I've been flying so many years now, I really am used to it." He settled back even more comfortably in his seat, his head resting against the back, but his eyes turned sideways to watch her. "All the same, I get that scary feeling when they take off – and I'll tell you something else. I like it. It makes it more interesting. It's the same feeling kids get on a roller coaster, I guess – and that's what makes it great. The first time you fly – well, yes, that's not so great, but I promise you you'll like it all a lot better on the way back. I mean – take this flight now. We're way over those clouds already, and you never noticed us get there, hmm?"

She turned her head to look out of her window again, and there below her – but not too far below this time – was a great bubbling curling expanse of white, with tinges of grey and pink where the sun shadowed it into curving patterns.

"Looks like cottage cheese, doesn't it?" he said and his voice sounded even more relaxed. "Real appetizing."

"Er – yes. Very pretty," she said. "And – er – thank you."

"Oh, it was a pleasure. I've talked a lot of people up in my time." He grinned widely, and his face creased into a map of friendliness. "Now, let me complete the therapy and buy you a drink when that little air hostess lady gets to us. I'd recommend champagne – "

"Oh – no, no thank you – " she said, suddenly embarrassed. Ye Gods, her mind whispered at her. Not five minutes out of sight of home and you're letting strange

2

Americans offer you champagne! "I'll not bother you. Very kind, but – "

"Should I have suggested whisky, then?" he smiled even more widely if that were possible. "As a good Scot, perhaps you find the idea of champagne a bit too soft and southern?"

"Not at all!" she said, and knew the stiffness had come back to her voice. "I'd just rather not have a drink at all, thanks all the same."

"Now, you're offended!" he said, quite unabashed. "Because I spotted you were a Scot? Notice I didn't say Scotch – I know better than that. A Scot or Scottish, isn't that the right way to say it? Mustn't say Scotch, on account that's the name of the stuff you drink. Ah, now, be friendly! Let me buy you a drink, just for company's sake. We're going to be here side by side for another hour or more – you can't expect me to sit here like an Englishman, all tight and stiff, now can you?"

He unbuckled his belt, and turned towards her, holding out one hand.

"Let me introduce myself properly. I'm Bartholomew Squires, Biff to my friends, hailing from Buffalo, New York, on my way to Palma on business. I'm with a property development firm – we're building flats out there in Majorca for middle-aged middle-Western widow ladies to retire to on the proceeds of their husband's heart attacks. Now, it's your turn," and he held his head to one side, and smiled his broad very white-toothed smile again.

She hesitated for a moment, feeling all the tension of the past weeks building up in her. I don't want to get involved again – But then her native good sense reared up, and the little voice in the corner of her mind hissed at her "Don't be so daft, girl! He's just a friendly man from a friendly country – you don't have to get *involved*", and she put her own hand out and they shook hands a little solemnly.

3

"I'm Isabel Cameron. From a little clachan – village – not far from Glasgow. I'm on my way to Palma to a job. How do you do."

"How do you do," he said gravely. "And what sort of job, or would you rather not say?"

"A – oh – a hotel job."

"A hotel job! Well, that's original, I guess. Who doesn't work in the tourist business in the Balearics? Mind, you don't look like a chambermaid or a barmaid or a – ?"

She laughed then. "You really like to know, don't you? Very American of you. All right, I'm not going to be a barmaid or a chambermaid – and you probably know perfectly well that they don't employ foreigners for jobs like that! – I'm a nurse. I'm going to be the resident nurse at a hotel just outside Palma. Looking after the residents and their children, and that sort of thing."

"A nurse? Well, now that really is something! Let me tell you all about my symptoms – " and he laughed aloud at the alarmed look that leapt into her face. "Isn't that what they all say?"

"Yes, that's what they all say." She smiled herself then. "And I usually shut them up by telling them to get undressed so that I can examine them."

"Oh, I like that! That's a beautiful ploy – ah, now, here's our nice hostess! Now, good morning to you. What sort of offerings has that portable bar of yours got?"

Isabel turned her head to look out of the window again, leaving him to his bantering chatter with the girl in the yellow uniform, gazing down at the clouds below her. The sky was an agonizing blue in the vivid sunshine and she was grateful for the dark glasses she had put on before she left the hotel that morning. She'd put them on then to hide the state of her eyes; they had been red-rimmed and a little swollen, which wasn't very surprising. You can't cry half the night and not

4

look like a smashed pudding, she had thought bitter-
ly.

She was aware for a moment of the voices beside her,
the chatter about champagne and duty free cigars, and
then pushed the sound away. She shouldn't have let this
wretched American beguile her as he had; she'd made up
her mind, right from the start, that she was going to stay
locked up inside herself for the whole of the summer. This
job was to be therapy, and she was going to do nothing
but work. No friendships, no involvements with anybody,
especially not with personable men. She'd had enough,
and there were wounds to be healed before she would
risk any such thing again. And already, here was a man
buying her a drink. Oh, damn, damn, damn, she thought,
and shook her head slightly in irritation.

"You don't have to talk if you don't want to, of
course."

She started, and looked at him, and he was smiling at
her.

"I can see you've a lot to think about, and I'll quite
understand if you prefer to be quiet."

"That's very obliging of you," she said a little tartly.
"If a bit surprising. You went to a lot of trouble to start
me talking, and now you – "

"You've a very speaking sort of face, you know," he
said. "Even behind those great brown goggles. I could see
you were scared when we took off, so I talked to you to
get you over it. Now I can see you're – what's the word? –
oh, a bit hungup, I guess. So – " he shrugged. "You don't
have to talk if you don't want to. Not all Americans are
pushy louts, you know."

She reddened a little. "I wasn't thinking any such thing.
But – "

"But you'd rather be quiet. So, okay! – ah, here's our
drinks. Now, try this – "

5

The hostess put a small green bottle with a silver foil wrapper round its neck in front of her, and very carefully Biff Squires poured its contents into the plastic beaker that came with it, and then poured his own.

"Salud!" he murmured, raising his glass.

"What? Oh – slanjy va!" and she let herself relax again for a moment.

"There's a phrase! Is that the Scottish equivalent of Cheers, prosit, and the rest of it?"

"It is," she gulped some of the champagne and it tasted fresh and crisp and she enjoyed the sting of the bubbles against her tongue. "Thank you. This is very nice."

"Very nice," he said solemnly, and for a while they sat and sipped, as she looked out of the window at the so-slowly moving clouds, now parting into thinner shreds to reveal a faintly wrinkled bluish greyness very far below.

"That's the English Channel," Biff said after a while. "Not long now before we get over France, and then there'll be the Pyrenees. That's a glorious sight when the sky is clear – you'll like that – "

She was beginning to relax more and more, as the bubbles of the champagne slid away from her tongue to warm her belly and then spread to her arms and legs. She felt her shoulders soften, and the muscles of her neck and face lost some of their tightness, and without thinking she pulled off the sunglasses, which were heavy on her nose, to lean back against her seat, feeling better than she had for days.

"Now, that's more like it," he said softly. "With eyes as green as yours it's a sin and a crime to hide them."

She turned her head on the squabs of the seat to look at him a little owlishly.

" – and they go very well with that hair of yours. I

6

thought it was the Irish that went in for green eyes and curly red hair, not the Scots."

"Mr. Squires," she said, and her voice was crisp and clear in her own ears. "I am most appreciative of your kindness. I *was* scared when we took off, and I suppose I *do* feel better now you've made me drink this. But that does not give you the right to make personal remarks, even though they're meant to be complimentary. So if you want to talk, just keep off the – the – chatting-up stuff, all right?"

"Whoa? That's me flattened to a pumpkin pie," he said, looking a little startled. "Okay, Isabel – or would you prefer Miss Cameron? – I'll watch myself. And I do apologize."

"There's no need," she said, a little pompously, and turned her head away to the window again.

But she couldn't stay so reserved for very long. The planeful of people was now much noisier, as the holiday making families settled down to talk to each other of hotels and plans for trips and the children began to bustle up and down the narrow central aisle to investigate the lavatories, and the hostesses served little plastic trays of sandwiches and cake and coffee. Almost before she realized it, they were talking again, as he told her of his plans for the next few months.

"I'm lucky to have been sent on this particular job," he said. "The old man usually sends me on domestic work – you know, Florida, California, and the rest of it. But our Spanish expert went sick, and this Majorcan job had to be done, so here I am! He had to let me go, seeing I was the only one left who spoke Spanish. I majored in languages at College, so he couldn't argue!"

"The old man? Your boss?" she murmured, not really very interested. The combination of champagne and the warmth of the sun coming through the windows was

7

making her very sleepy. And she had slept so little the night before –

"Er – you could call him that." He looked at her a little sharply, and opened his mouth as though to say more but then closed it, and they sat in silence for a while.

"Look!" he said suddenly, and she opened her eyes, which had closed in response to the sleepiness that was filling her, and she followed his pointing finger to the window. And then caught her breath with the glory of what she saw.

Great soaring brown peaks were thrusting through the shreds of cotton wool clouds to outline themselves against the intense blue of the sky, their tips shrouded in froths of blindingly white snow. From each iced peak runnels of white ran down, bubbling softly into crevasses and out to ledges before thinning out again as they disappeared further down into the softer greenness of the lower slopes. The plane seemed to be standing still with just the edge of the wing she could see in front of her trembling slightly; but the mountains seemed to move with an awesome majestic slowness, creeping past the sunlit window like a private army provided for her review. She craned her head a little to see further and there, far, far ahead of the plane, peak after peak unfolded icing sugar dusted tips in the crisp light to march away and gradually disappear into the far haze of the horizon. And she found her eyes filled with tears and her throat tight as she stared and stared, trying to print the images permanently onto her memory.

"It is extraordinary, isn't it?" Biff said softly. "It made me want to cry the first time I saw it. People are so unimportant, aren't they, when you look at the Pyrenees?"

She nodded, unwilling to speak, and then leaned back in her seat to close her eyes again, ashamed of the tears that stood in them, afraid they would spill over and make her look a fool in front of this man.

He seemed to be aware of her need for silence, and said nothing, though she was very conscious of the warmth of his square body beside her, and found it oddly comforting.

"You mustn't," she thought. "You mustn't get involved, you mustn't need anyone ever again. You can't. You're tired, and you're over-excited and that damned champagne – remember you mustn't – you mustn't – "

The sounds around her pulsed heavily, the buzzing of the engines, the voices of excited passengers pointing out the view to each other, the high shrill voices of the children; and then the pulsing thickened and spread to fill her whole body and she knew she was falling asleep, and let it happen.

But she dreamed again, not the same dream exactly, for now the mountains were part of it. She was climbing with agonizing slowness, each foot feeling dead and heavy as she tried to lift it, and far ahead and above her she could see him, Jason, his hands in his pockets and his white coat flying behind him as he leapt easily from peak to peak; never quite out of sight, sometimes seeming closer as she tried to catch him. She called him, hopelessly, and he turned and wavcd cheerfully and then leapt on and again she called, making her mouth shape his name. "Jay! – Jay – wait for me! Please don't make me go away – Jay – "

And then, suddenly, she was awake, to find Biff's hand on her shoulder, and an anxious expression that looked oddly incongruous on his wide freckled face.

"What's the matter?" she said stupidly. "What – "

"That's what I was wondering," he said softly. "You were thrashing about a bit, you know? And calling out, so I – well – " he looked over his shoulder and she saw the air hostess leaning across to look worriedly at her. "I

9

thought you'd rather I woke you before you – before too many people noticed."

"Thank you," she said, and shook her head a little to clear it. "I'm sorry – I was dreaming – "

"Not to worry," he said, and leaned back in his seat again, and the air hostess asked her if she wanted anything and went away when Isabel shook her head, and after a moment or two she said awkwardly, "That was – I'm sorry about that. I do dream a little – loudly – sometimes, I'm told."

"Are you?" he said noncommittally, and then she blushed a violent red, and fumbled for her handbag on the floor beside her. "I think I'll just go and tidy myself – " she mumbled, and immediately he got up and made way for her, and she hurried along the narrow aisle to lock herself gratefully into the tiny lavatory.

She sat on the edge of the basin for a moment, her hot cheeks between her hands, and then, as the tears started to climb up into her throat again with sickening familiarity, turned sharply to fill the basin with cold water and wash her face. She scrubbed it dry, and then with hands a little clumsy with tension, began to pull makeup from her bag.

Her face looked lugubriously back at her from the small mirror, and she stared at her reflection consideringly.

"Ah, look at you, girl!" she whispered. "Daft as a brush! Will you stop being so sorry for yourself? So it's over. O-V-E-R. Over. He behaved fair and square, didn't he? You knew when it started that there were no promises in it. He never promised anything – "

But that made no difference. As she spread fresh foundation over her pale cheeks, filling the hollows under her eyes with colour, and then swept a little pale green shadow on to her reddened lids, she knew that no amount of talking sense to herself would make her feel much better.

10

Only time could do that. The memories came sweeping into her, and now she made no attempt to stem them.

A year. A year since Jason Chandos had come to the Royal as a Surgical Registrar, a year since that Sunday afternoon in the operating theatre where she had been preparing the week's operating lists and he had come to "look round".

"I always come and chat up the theatre sister," he had said gaily. "Self-preservation, that. Get the Lady of the Knife on your side, and you're home and dry, first thing a young surgeon learns. I'm lucky this time – you are a doll, do you know that? You should have seen the theatre sister at St. Dominics, now, my last job. She was the absolute end – but you look – oh, I'm going to enjoy this job, that's for sure – "

She had answered him pertly enough, used to the sort of chat young doctors liked to produce for nursing staff, but she had found herself surprisingly affected by him. Not his good looks; he wasn't particularly good looking, really, she had decided, watching him as he sat there perched easily on the edge of the operating table, his hands thrust into his trouser pockets under his white coat, his face alight with amusement as he talked. Dark brown hair, a bit rumpled, a narrow lipped mouth that was almost alarmingly interesting, dark blue eyes that looked very directly at her. But not classic good looks, attractive though he was.

Attractive. She thought of the word now, rolling it round in her mind as she carefully brushed mascara onto her lashes. What did it mean, after all? Just that he was the most exciting man she'd ever met. That was all. Within a month they were going out together regularly, and within three months she had surrendered all attempts at pretending she wasn't hopelessly, agonizingly in love with him.

11

Every time he had come into the theatres, it was as though the very walls of the place shook and lurched, as her belly contracted and her heart thumped. And when he touched her, kissed her – that had been the most devastating thing that had ever happened to her.

She remembered with an almost wry amusement the amazement she had felt; she, Isabel Cameron, cool sensible Isabel who had gone through her training days heart-whole and lightly remote from the torrid to-ings and fro-ings of the rest of her set. They fell in love and out of it as often as they had hot dinners, as she had told them often enough when they teased her about the medical students who obviously yearned after her, but got no more than a cool dismissing stare from her level green eyes. She, to fall so helplessly in love! It was a judgement on her, that was what it was. But even though she knew she was being as soft as a bairn she had let it happen. Let herself become more and more dependent on him for all her living, for her emotional needs, her intellectual needs, her physical needs. Above all, her physical needs. But that memory she had to push away, carefully concentrating on painting lipstick onto her stretched lips in an effort to control the shiver of feeling that rose in her as she remembered his arms about her, his mouth hard on hers –

And now it was over. He had told her honestly, and with obvious distress, that he'd thought about it all very carefully, and love her in his own way though he did, it wasn't in her way, and she deserved better.

"I know what's right for you, Isabel, and I care too much for you to go on like this. I'm not the marrying kind – if I know nothing else about myself I know that. And this – this arrangement – it's unfair to you – "

"But I'm not asking you to marry me, man!" she had cried. "When did I ever do that? I just want you, and if I tell you I don't care about anything else as long as you love me and we're together why should you want to change things? Don't you – don't you enjoy our – being with me, the way we are? Or are you really trying to tell me you love someone else – that you're tired of me?"

"It's not that – I just don't think it's right to go on like this – not married, nor intending to be, but – "

He'd shrugged then. "It's all right for me, but not for you. Not in the long run. You'd be better off forgetting me and finding someone who *would* be right for you – someone who'd look after you and settle down and – "

It had gone on and on, the talking, the explaining, the discussing, until she was almost pleading with him, begging him to go on loving her, however little – it was enough just to be able to love him, to make love, to be together –

But it had made no difference, and in her pain and misery she had fled, leaving the Royal and Jason as far behind her as she could, taking this summer job in the sun of a Mediterranean resort, so that she could be free of her love for him.

"But you brought yourself with you, didn't you?" she murmured at her reflection, and then grimaced, remembering the way she had lain in bed at the hotel last night, weeping and twisting from side to side, aching for him, sick with loss and anger and misery. She had thought in her stupid way, that just going away would be enough. The interest of a new job in a new place would be enough to get rid of Jason for good and all. Yet she had dreamt about him here, on the plane, on the way to her new experiences –

"The hell with it!" she thought, with a sudden flash of anger. "You're a stupid fool, Isabel Cameron, that you are. Wallowing in your misery like some green girl! Grow up and be your age. At twenty three you should know better! Now, go back to your seat and be nice to that Biff man, and let him date you if he wants to. You're going

13

to Majorca to have fun, not to pine after Jason bloody Chandos, right? Right."

With her head held high and her neck stiff she marched back to her seat, to buckle herself into her safety belt and ply a rather startled Biff with vivacious questions about the island, about Spanish customs, Spanish food and drink, and Spanish people. And by the time they landed, curling in over the windmills and cactuses and dusty pink and white houses of the plains that lay south of the island's spine of mountains, she had agreed to have dinner with him at a barbecue in the country some time.

And by the time he had guided her expertly through passport control and customs, dealing effortlessly with the chatter of the blue overalled porters and the bustle of the crowded echoing halls of the airport, she felt much better. She had embarked on a new experience, an interesting experience, a fun experience, and she was going to enjoy it if it killed her.

14

2

She stood in the wide hallway of the hotel, blinking a little as her eyes grew accustomed to the dimness, for the light in the streets through which her taxi had driven her had been very strong.

She was dazed with the impact of so much that was strange. Strange sights of course – bright sunshine in February, when the England she had left behind had been so grey, was very startling to the eyes. So were the peeling and dusty terracotta and pink and white buildings with their tightly closed green shutters, the palm trees sitting squat to the ground, the great pile of masonry that was the cathedral rising haughtily above the town, the policemen in dull khaki-coloured uniforms with gun holsters on their hips, and the dark green foliage of trees amidst which vivid gleams of colour showed the presence of lemons and oranges. Strange smells too, a dusty hot smell, and unusual but appetizing wafts from restaurants, wine and fish and fruit and oil. And the sounds, the loud lisping chatter of Spanish, and the screech of brakes which had terrified her as her taxi bucketed her from the airport, but which was, it seemed, normal on the island for every vehicle produced the noise as it leapt round corners; it was all almost overwhelming.

She took a deep breath now and as she grew accustomed to the new quality of light looked around her. And widened her eyes with surprise as she took it all in. She had

15

never seen anything quite so picture-book-luxurious in her life before; the broad foyer in which she was standing was floored with marble, gleaming softly in the light thrown from the far windows. The windows spread fully across the wall, some sixty feet wide framing a view of the Bay with its dancing white-flecked blue water, red and white triangles of sails on fishing boats, nests of masts clustered at the edges, a sweep of shoreline edged with skyscraper hotel buildings that looked for all the world as though they were built of a child's toy bricks.

The view was muted, however, for each window was shrouded in swathes of delicate blue but half transparent curtaining which gave the light the gentle dim quality that was so very relaxing to her eyes. In the great area of marble between the windows and the place where she stood were scattered clumps of furniture, huge leather covered sofas and deep armchairs, separated by long low tables on which bowls of flowers, arranged with consummate artistry, stood in elegant perfection. And the pictures on the walls, great canvases showing still lifes, and scornfully beautiful women and leaping horses and then the sculptures that stood in niches against the double row of marble pillars that marched across the hall towards great double doors at the far end – it was all so incredibly *rich*.

The doors were open and she could see beyond them into the restaurant to tables covered with gleaming white cloths and sparkling glass and silver, and people eating and laughing and drinking, and even from this distance she could see that these people were rich. The clothes she could see looked expensive, the women's makeup and hairdressing looked expensive, even the children – and there were several – looked expensive.

Somewhere deep inside herself a soft giggle began to rise; she, Isabel, daughter of a canny Scots farmer, brought up to be suspicious of any fripperies and non-senses of the sort that those effete Southerners went in for, to be spending a long summer in a place so outrageously, showily, unashamedly as extravagant as this hotel. It was ridiculous, and she could just imagine how her father would have looked if he had been alive to see her here. And the giggle exploded softly against her teeth, and came out as a snort of amusement.

Somewhere behind her there was a soft sound in answer, and she whirled to look, and now saw against the far wall, beside the smoked glass doors to the street, the reception desk. When her taxi driver had set her down she had just walked straight in, looking neither to right nor left, and she reddened now, feeling very foolish, for there was a man leaning across the desk, watching her with his face filled with amusement.

"Señorita – er – Cameron? Buenas tardes? Me alegro de verle – ah – entiende usted español? You comprehend Spanish?"

She swallowed, and then very carefully, her tongue tripping a little on the strange syllables, she said, "Uh – Io hablo un poco – "

"Ah – you speak a little – but you prefer I speak English, si? So – I am very happy to see you. I am waiting a little time for you, because I sent the hotel driver to the airport but the man comes back without you – he meets the wrong plane. Qué disparate, verdad? So, perdóneme, I am sorry and I welcome you to Majorca. And to the Hotel Cadiz. It is very beautiful, verdad? Is it not?"

"Er – very beautiful – " and then, a little shyly added, "Me gusta – "

"You like it! I am delighted. Very happy. Now I intro-duce myself, hmm? I am Jaime Mendoza, the manager of this hotel. We work together very close, yes?"

He came out from behind the desk, and now she could

17

see him more clearly. A slight man – not much taller than herself, so about five foot five – with a classic Spanish look to him, dapper, neatly dressed, dark sleek hair, tanned sallow skin and dark eyes. He looked at her with such clear admiration on his face that for a moment she felt a tingle of annoyance and then realizing how absurd the reaction was, put out her hand towards him with more warmth than she would normally have displayed.

"Mucho Gusto, Señor Mendoza."

He held her hand a moment longer than she really liked, smiling at her very charmingly. "Please to call me Jaime – you can pronounce it your English way? *Ch* – it is a difficult sound for the English – "

"But not for a Scot," she said, gently extricating her hand. "We use the same sound – like in Sassenach – Ch-ey-me – isn't that it ?"

"Yes! exactly right!" He positively sparkled his delight at her. "Exactly! But of course, there are close contacts, between Spain and Scotland in the history, yes? I remember I learn at school. So, you call me Jaime, as you are a *special* member of our staff. The others – " he lifted his shoulders a little pompously "the other staff must call me Señor, of course. But you will be different. Now, you are called – ?"

"Er – Isabel," she said, feeling more and more uncomfortable. Damn it, this little man *was* making a pass at her! It wasn't just her imagination. Two in one day – this was getting ridiculous.

"But a grand way to get over a spoiled love affair, you'll grant that," whispered her private voice a little wickedly.

"Isabella! Sin Mentera! A name of Spain, you know that?"

"I'd forgotten till now," Isabel said a little dryly, and then turned towards the door. "Er – my luggage – it's out there – the taxi driver left it."

"Ah, of course – of course. So, I find a porter – "

He bustled back to his desk, and disappeared into the room behind it, and she heard him call "José! Sirvace hacer subir equipaje la Señorita Cameron!" and was childishly pleased to find she understood what he said. Have the luggage of Miss Cameron taken up – the few weeks she had spent listening to Spanish records was going to prove very useful. But then, as a porter appeared, talking volubly and Mendoza talked even more volubly back, she realized that her grasp of the language was virtually nil, for she hardly understood one word in a hundred.

At last the porter, shrugging, went away to collect her luggage, and Mendoza muttering "Es una cara dura – " took a key from the board behind him, and came hurrying back to her, once more wreathed in smiles.

"Such troubles we have with these porters – they hate to work, you know? But he is not so bad a man, after all. I can handle these people. Now, come, I show you your room, and tell you of the way the work is for you, yes?"

The lift was huge and mirror-bedecked and thickly carpeted and once more Isabel wanted to laugh at the absurd luxury of it all; and realized that she was more tired than she knew as once more a soft snort escaped her.

Mendoza looked at her sharply, and then smiled widely. "You are happy to be with us, yes? I am delighted – me alegro – you will be happy with us. And we will be happy with you – this I know," and he reached across to squeeze her arm above the elbow, and she reddened, grateful that the lift arrived at the same moment.

"This is the top floor, a special section for special staff – I have my own little apartment up here, too, yes?" He bustled ahead of her, along thickly carpeted corridors lined with heavy doors, the walls again decorated with pictures, and a chambermaid in a crisp white uniform put

19

her head out of a door to stare at them as they went by, bobbing back quickly at the sight of Mendoza.

"You see?" he said smugly, smiling at her in high good humour. "Me they are alarmed to see. Which is good for the hotel, yes? You of course, are different, verdad?" and again he smiled at her, and again she felt embarrassed.

"Tell me about the work," she said quickly as he reached a door at the far end of the corridor, and fumbled the key into the lock. "The nurse before me – why did she leave?"

She had asked the employment agency in London which had appointed her about this, but they didn't know. All they could tell her was that the job was for the six months of the season, well paid, and with accommodation thrown in. Her employer was Señor Garcia, the owner of the hotel, and he would answer her questions, the girl at the agency had said. And desperate as she was to get away, and glad to get any offer of a job abroad without a true grasp of the language, Isabel had seized the opportunity and the job, risking it being a disappointment. Even that would be better than staying at the Royal near Jason.

"Oh, there was no nurse before you," Mendoza said cheerfully. "This is why I am so very interested in you coming. It is a very new idea, this, of Señor Garcia." He looked at her sharply. "You have met Señor Garcia?"

"No, not yet."

"Ah." He leaned against the wall, and folded his arms, looking at her very solemnly. "I must tell you he is a – he is a very difficult man. If you have problems, you should not to him talk. No. It is better to come always to me, as I am the manager, verdad? Yes? It is better always to come to me." He put his hand out and realizing he was aiming once again for her arm she moved adroitly, and pushed against the door.

"This is my room? How nice – "

20

He stepped forward so that she couldn't pass him. "I tell you why there is no nurse before you, yes? Until now, Señor Garcia did not think we required so special a person. If we have illness, which the Good God should forbid, we send for a doctor. But last summer, there is trouble. We have much illness in the hotel, much problems, Señora Garcia says – no more. Next summer, Sebastian, she says, you have una enfermera – a nurse – she says! So, of course, Señor Garcia arranges it so!"

"Señora? He's married, then?"

"Oh, no – not Señor Garcia! He is like me – a man alone – a bachelor." He leered cheerfully at her. "No, the Señora is the mother of Señor Garcia. Such a woman – they say in France, une femme formidable! You see, in my job I must be a speaker of many languages!"

"Indeed, you are a remarkable linguist," Isabel said solemnly and he nodded at her in great good humour, and at last stood back to let her into her room as the porter appeared at the end of the corridor, humping her luggage on a small trolley.

"You like this, yes?" Mendoza said, sweeping the door open, and she walked past him to stand delightedly looking around. A square room, with cool yellow curtains drawn against the afternoon sunshine, a carpet of a deeper yellow, a wide low bed with a counterpane in yet another shade of the golden colour, and walls of very soft cream. There were fitted wardrobes which she opened and exclaimed over, so well equipped were they with drawers and mirrors and lights, and a charming little bathroom with a shower and bath and bidet – "And a loo all to myself – that's almost indecent luxury!" she murmured, and laughed at his expression of surprise.

"It's a lovely room, Señor Mendoza – "

"Jaime!"

"I'm sorry – Jaime. Delightful. Thank you, and thank

Señor Garcia for arranging such excellent accommodation. I – er – " another of her painfully learned Spanish phrases was dredged up, " – er – le estoy muy agradecido – is that right? I am much obliged to you."

"Excellent, excellent! Soon you will be a linguist like myself, yes? Now, if you require anything, you ring for la criada – the maid – and she provides. I must return to the office – soon the guests come out from lunch and then – qué aburrido!" – he raised his right hand and shook it limply from the wrist in a very characteristic Spanish fashion – "They torment me, they want this, they want that, they are impossible! So, when you are ready, you come down, and I arrange for you a cup of English tea, and then we discuss your duties, and I show you the clinic we have prepared for you, yes? Hasta la vista, señorita!" and he bowed rather comically, and went away leaving her to unpack and arrange the room that was to be her home for the next six months.

She took a shower as soon as she had finished and after a little thought, put on the uniform she had provided for herself; the girl in the agency had been very vague about uniform too, so Isabel had thought it prudent to provide her own, to be on the safe side. Now, as she looked at herself in the crisp white nylon dress she had chosen, and the white tights and shoes the uniform shop had recommended ("so much better for tropical climes, Sister," the little elderly assistant had cooed so she had taken them) and the neat white "Sister Dora" cap firmly clipped to her crisp red hair, she knew she looked every inch the nurse, if rather like one of the American variety.

Which reminded her of Biff, and she smiled a little as she tidied away the odds and ends of makeup and her bathroom gear, ready to go downstairs. Bruised and miserable though she felt about Jason, and determined though she still was to avoid any further emotional

22

entanglements, there was a certain comfort to be found in having a date with a new man, to know he'd found her interesting enough to want to see her again.

She drew the curtains before she left, meaning to open the window wide, for the room seemed too warm and to her delight found there was a balcony outside, and that it overlooked the sea side of the hotel. Eagerly she stepped out to peer over the edge, and caught her breath in a moment of terror.

She was on the eleventh floor of the building, only a glassed-in dome on the roof behind her being higher than she was, and the hotel itself was perched on the edge of a cliff that dropped sharply down to the waters of the Bay beneath. Below her, series of balconies just like her own were repeated in a dizzying pattern, all the way down to the glass roof of the restaurant, below which she could see the foreshortened figures of a few late lunchers and the white jacketed waiters clearing tables.

Beyond that, and thrusting forward from the terrace which she could see ran round the edge of the restaurant was a shelf of garden, in the middle of which lay a very blue, very still swimming pool, a curving sinuous thing shaped like an elongated kidney. It was surrounded by long lounging chairs with gay red and blue and yellow canopies over them, and a few mattresses with brightly striped covers lay about on the paving stones with people lying on them, browning gently in the sun, which felt to Isabel as warm as an English May afternoon.

She let her eyes wander further, trying to take in the extent of this huge hotel, and saw there was another swimming pool to the far side of the kidney shaped one, but this was obviously for children for she could see gay pictures of dolphins and octopuses and cheeky lobsters patterned on the tiled floor under the blue green water;

23

and a small brown figure wearing a diminutive swimsuit was paddling at one end.

And there were still more chair bedecked terraces, more gardens gleaming with red and purple flowers, and mimosa trees, and orange and lemon trees, and glossy dark green foliage lying spread about under this great slab of a building with its balconies looking rather like rows of eyelashes – at which simile, Isabel went into her room again, and firmly closed the window.

"I'm getting fanciful, and that'll never do," she told herself tartly. "You're here to work, not to get a taste for the high and expensive jet-set life – and don't you forget it."

But all the same, it was going to be an interesting summer, and a very comfortable one, she thought as she hurried along the quiet corridor towards the lift. "I've done the right thing coming here – it *will* be all right for me, now. I know it will. It's got to be!"

3

Jaime Mendoza was so patently waiting for her at the desk in the main hall, and so patently trying to pretend that he wasn't that she wanted to laugh, especially as at the sight of her emerging from the lift he immediately began to scold the little dark haired girl sitting at a desk in the corner behind him.

"Señor Mendoza!" she interrupted him without compunction, feeling very sorry for the little typist who was obviously being made to suffer simply to provide Mendoza with a chance to show off. "You told me to come to you as soon as I was unpacked – "

"Ah, Isabella! It is all comfortable with you, yes?" he beamed at her and came hurrying round the desk to stand close beside her. "Now, I arrange for you some tea, and show you the clinic we have prepare for you – "

"Thank you," she said equably, and then moving away from his rather oppressive closeness added, "And Señor Garcia? When do I see him? I understood I was to report to him when I arrived, so – "

"Ah, yes. Señor Garcia. I arrange very soon. He does not like to be interrupted too early in the afternoon – the desk work, you understand – "

"Hey, Manager!"

Isabel turned her head to see a tall woman in very tight pale blue pants and a white silk sweater bearing down on them. Her hair was very golden, even in the gentle light of the foyer, and piled on top of her head in carefully arranged casual confusion. Half her suntanned face was hidden by huge square dark glasses.

"Manager, what the devil is the matter with that stupid creature who is supposed to be the head waiter here? Three times – *three*, no less – I had to send back a dish, and when I complained to him about it and about the stupid table waiter all that man did was shrug at me in a very ill mannered fashion and disappear! And I won't have it, do you understand? At the price this hotel charges I do not expect to be treated with such impudence. If it happens once more, I promise you I won't be nearly so lenient. This time I'm telling you – next time I tell Mr. Garcia. Now, you go and talk to that man and see to it that he apologizes to me when I go in to dinner – "

"Felipe was impudent? Surely not, Señora – "

She took her glasses off with a flick of her wrist that showed very clearly the large diamond ring that adorned one finger and stared at him with her eyebrows raised and her eyes slightly narrowed.

"Are you calling me a liar, Manager? I – "

"But, Señora, of course not! I am merely surprised – very surprised that Felipe, who is, I assure you, an excellent head waiter, should behave in any way that was not – " he shrugged "and to so – so happy a guest! You must agree, he is always of the most correct? Usually?"

"But not today. So are you going to deal with the matter or must I discuss it with Mr. Garcia – "

"I see at once, Señora – excuse me, please. I return soon – " And he bustled away leaving Isabel still standing beside the tall woman.

"And who might you be?" the woman said, flicking her eyes across the crisp uniform and back to Isabel's face. "You aren't Spanish."

"No, I'm not Spanish," Isabel said quietly.

26

"Then who are you? I've been staying here months and I haven't seen *you* before. You're a nurse aren't you? Someone ill here? Because if there's any infection in the place, you can be sure I – "

"Nobody is ill," Isabel said in the same quiet voice, but feeling her irritation rising. She'd met people like this before; bad tempered, spoiled, and rich. The Royal's Private Patients' wing had more than its fair share of such difficult people to deal with. "I am a nurse, yes, but no one is ill. Señor Garcia decided to provide health services for his guests, so – "

"Well, well! We are getting up-to-date, aren't we? I must tell him I approve! Where will you be if you're wanted? There are one or two things I daresay I could get you to deal with for me – do I just ring the desk when I want you?"

"I really don't know yet. I've only just arrived and I haven't yet seen the clinic room I'll be using. But if you should be *ill* then of course, a call to the desk will be the best way of finding me. I hope you won't need me, however. One wouldn't want to think of people's holidays being spoiled by genuine ill health – "

The woman raised her eyebrows again, and the sun-tanned skin of her cheeks creased into sharp lines; "she's a lot older than she looks,"

Isabel thought, looking at the other woman with her own face set in carefully noncommittal lines. "Older and very, very difficult. I'll have to watch this one – "

But the woman contented herself with a sharp sniff, and said only, "Yes, it would. But I'm not on holiday. I'm spending the whole season here. My name is Connaught – Mrs. Vanda Connaught. You'll know who I am now, when I send for you, won't you?" and she thrust her glasses back on to her nose and went hipping away towards the lift, moving with a studied languorousness that Isabel found rather embarrassing on a woman who was obviously nearer fifty than forty.

Jaime Mendoza came hurrying back from the dining room, his face creased with anxiety. "That woman!" he said breathlessly. "She is so much trouble, always trouble, trouble, trouble! Felipe in a rage, half the waiters shouting and swearing in the kitchen – she spends every meal time upsetting everybody – qué fastidio! – such a nuisance of a woman! But what can you do? She is rich, she spends much in the bar, and Señor Garcia – " he shrugged very expressively. "Well, you will see – you will see! Now, the tea, and I show you the clinic!"

He showed a disposition to linger over the tea, which they had at a table in the corner of the vast restaurant, but she did her best to be businesslike and crisp with him, drinking the tea – which was thin and lemon scented and very refreshing – and eating the soft and very delicious sweet biscuits that came with it as quickly as she decently could. He also showed a disposition to try to talk to her in rather personal terms, asking her about life at home, about the sort of city London was, and – a little slyly – about her boyfriends. But she parried his questions adroitly by asking him her own about the hotel.

"This restaurant is very magnificent," she said, looking up at the vast sweep of glass above their heads, through which she could see the sheer side of the hotel rising hugely above them. "But very hot, I should think when the sun is strong? Today is pleasant and bright, but in the high summer, surely? – "

"Ah, this is a very special roof!" he said proudly, and lifting one hand imperiously signalled the young white jacketed waiter who was hovering at the serving table nearby. "We demonstrate – "

The waiter had moved away to the far corner of the great room, and was fiddling with some switches, and suddenly, as she stared upwards, the whole roof changed as sheets of green canvas crept up the panes like some immense umbrella operating in reverse. Within seconds the whole area was plunged into a cool shimmering under-sea sort of greenness, and she shivered a little as a waft of cool air moved across her shoulders and cheeks.

"You see? We have this unique – quite unique – system of sunblinds, and they operate in this special way – at the same time as the blinds come, so comes the cool air – you feel it, all the breathing of ice? It is scented like the air of the mountains, and even on the hottest days of August in here our guests sit in ease and comfort and feel no heaviness of the sun. It is remarkable, yes?"

"Remarkable very much yes!" she said, as the blinds began to creep silently down the panes again, so that the restaurant was again flooded with the light of the afternoon sun. "Indeed, this is a very comfortable hotel – and very thoughtful for its guests. Even providing a nurse for them – almost as special as the blinds, that!"

She stood up, and smoothed her uniform tidily. "And now, perhaps you'll take me to the clinic? I really feel I ought to see it and get myself organized as soon as possible. If one of the guests needed me and I wasn't ready for them, I'd not feel too happy about the situation! Er – thank you for my tea – "

"You eat in this dining room always, yes? You are a special member of the staff, so you do not eat in staff rooms, but like myself and like Señor Garcia, here in the restaurant where are the guests. It is a privilege for us who are the most important people of the hotel – "

The clinic was on the lower ground floor of the hotel beneath the foyer area, and reached through the magnificent library, a room so full of leather bound books, deep armchairs and writing desks that it almost defied use. To sit at one of these desks under one of those beautiful

29

paintings would, Isabel was sure, paralyse her so that she couldn't think a word, let alone write one.

For a moment she was afraid that the clinic also would be on too magnificent a scale, but she need not have worried. There were three small rooms. One was a waiting area, with chairs and table and magazines, and a small plant-entwined balcony of its own. Beyond that was a surgical room, and she gazed at it in delight, so fully equipped and gleaming was it.

Cabinets of chrome and glass lined the walls, all of them filled with rows of gleaming instruments, or bottles of lotions and antiseptics and drugs. There was a reclining chair with a head rest, rather like a dentist's chair – "for care of the eyes, the ears and such matters, yes?" Jaime said – as well as an operating table in the centre.

He gave her a bunch of keys with another of his little bows and she took them with a murmured "thank you" and began to look through the cabinets and was amazed to discover that not a single item she could imagine for the sort of emergencies or treatment she might have to give was missing.

"Who arranged all this?" she asked curiously, closing the last cabinet door and carefully pinning the small bunch of keys to her belt, in time-honoured chatelaine fashion. "Obviously it was someone who knew what it was all about – "

"Oh, yes. We sent to Madrid for advice, for all the equipment, and they arrange it specially. When Señor Garcia does a thing, he does it very well, I promise this!"

"Like the restaurant roof," she murmured, and went across to look into the last room in the clinic complex. This was a recovery room, with a comfortable couch, a couple of armchairs, and a desk in the corner on which lay charts and note folders. "So you can keep all necessary

30

records," Jaime said. "And here, you see, we provide a bag of equipment for you, in case you must see guests in their rooms. It is suitable for you?"

"Very suitable. Splendidly suitable! I'm near breathless with it. There're doctors at home who'd give their eyeteeth for such a setup!"

"Eyeteeth?" he wrinkled his face in puzzlement.

"It's no matter," she said. "Just a phrase – now, if it's all right with you, Señor – sorry Jaime – I'll stay here for a bit and get used to the set-up. You'll be able to contact me if you need me – " she indicated the phone on the desk, "So I'll not waste any more of your time. I daresay you've a great deal to do up there. Thank you again for your very kind welcome to me – "

He was away and out of the door almost before he realized she had made him go, and she breathed a sigh of relief once the door closed behind him; she was going to have to use a good deal of such skill as she had to keep this eager little man at arms' length. But she smiled a little as she went back to the surgical room; for all his bustle and absurdity there was something very endearing about him. He liked her, that was the main thing; starting a new job in a new country was never easy, and to have someone to turn to for help if she needed it was no bad thing.

She moved around the rooms for a while, arranging her splendid equipment in an order that more easily fitted her own working patterns, and covering the operating table with a sheet which she found in a well stocked linen cupboard in the recovery room. The table looked rather alarming in its clinical perfection and thinking of the susceptibilities of possibly nervous hotel guests, she felt it looked better decently shrouded.

Then, she sat down at the desk and taking one of the empty notebooks began to rule it out to make it ready to receive information about such patients as she might get.

31

She was enjoying herself; naturally an orderly person, she found much satisfaction in establishing a brand new clinic with a brand new system – her own – and she whistled softly between her teeth as she worked.

There was a faint clatter from the surgical room, and she raised her head and listened carefully. Someone was moving about in there, and she moved swiftly, remembering that the cabinets contained several potentially dangerous drugs, and that she had left them all unlocked after investigating them.

There was a man, a tall thin man with very dark hair, standing with his back to her and his head almost inside one of the cabinets, and she moved quickly across the room towards him.

"Señor! – what do you want? ah – " she struggled for a moment and then said loudly and slowly "Qué quiere usted? Qué hace usted aquî?"

"What am I doing here?" he said in slightly accented but very perfect English. "I am looking for something for this – " and he held out his hand towards her. It was bloody and automatically she put her own hand forwards to turn it palm downwards so that the blood did not drip on the floor.

"Come and sit down," she said crisply. "I'll see to it at once."

Obediently he sat in the chair, and watched her as she moved swiftly to the wash basin in the corner to scrub her hands before putting his hand on to a clean towel which she took from a metal drum of sterile dressings. She was aware of his eyes on her, and in her own turn took stock of him.

He had very dark eyes under straight silky black eyebrows, and a pale skin that slid into violet coloured shadows above his cheekbones and at his temples. Most startling of all was the neat beard which covered the point

32

of his chin and upper lip, sweeping up his cheeks to stop in a crisp line across them. It was startlingly silver on each side, only the very middle of it being as black as his hair, and it gave him a look that was slightly sardonic and yet weary.

She worked quickly, bringing a tray with a bowl of cleansing lotion and swabs and dressings, grateful she had had at least some time to find out where everything was. She would have felt a particular chagrin if she had shown herself in this odd man's eyes to be anything but fully competent, a response in herself which she found a little irritating.

It was a very ugly gash, running across the back of his hand in a ragged line and she looked at it with a faint frown.

"How did you do it?"

He shrugged. "I broke a glass. The edge – "

"A broken glass? On the *back* of your hand?"

"It was with the back of my hand that I broke it," he said calmly, lifting his heavy lids to look at her. "Like so – " and he moved his hand swiftly and it was as though she had seen the accident happen.

"I see! Was the glass clean or dirty?"

"Quite clean. It contained brandy. It was therefore virtually free of germs, yes? The spirit will have acted as an antiseptic."

"Hmm. Up to a point, maybe," she said. "I still think you should have some antibiotic on it, to be on the safe side. And I think you should have a few stitches in this, too. We'll have to find out about getting you to a doctor – "

"Can't you stitch it?" he was still looking at her with his heavy-lidded direct gaze, leaning back now in total relaxation in the chair. "I have not the time for going to doctors. You do it?"

33

"I?" she frowned. "Well, I'm quite capable, of course. I was a theatre sister before coming here, and I've done a good deal of this sort of work. But you – surely you'd prefer a doctor?"

"I've already told you I want you to do it." He dropped his eyes to look consideringly at his hand, still oozing blood across the knuckles, and he flexed his long fingers a little cautiously. "If you don't do it, it won't be done at all," he said then, and he looked up, smiling slightly. She realized almost with a shock that this was the first time his facial expression had changed since she had spoken to him.

"Very well, then," she said, making up her mind quickly. She had no doubts at all about her ability to make a good job of the suturing, and there was no sense in standing here arguing. So she covered the wound with a clean dressing, and moving with all the crispness of long experience began to prepare needles and nylon sutures and a syringe of local anaesthetic.

He said nothing at all as she worked, and the only sounds in the room were the clatter of her instruments as she slid them into the sterilizer and the hiss of the steam as she operated it. He made no sound either when she gave him the local anaesthetic, sliding the point of the needle into his skin at several points along the rim of the wound until it was surrounded with minute swellings where the liquid had collected.

"I'll not hurt you now – " she murmured as she started the suturing, carefully matching the edges at the centre of the wound to get as good a cosmetic result as possible. She had always taken a certain pride in her ability to suture a wound not merely adequately but in such a way that only the most minimal of scars remained; several of the Royal's surgeons had made a practice of relinquishing their place to her to do the surface stitching after operations.

As old Sir Jeffrey had said "Where's the sense in my

34

standing here struggling with a needle and thread in my great paws when here at my side stands a nimble fingered lass who's been wielding such articles all her life?" and he had winked at her and she had smiled back, for there was a special bond between the very old Scottish surgeon and the rather young Scottish sister.

Now, as she worked, she felt a moment of very poignant homesickness. She was back in her familiar operating theatre with the familiar sounds of the great traffic-heavy road leading down to London docks just outside and the great sprawling mass of buildings that was the old Royal –

But she wasn't; she was in a Spanish holiday resort with the Mediterranean lapping outside her windows, rather than the muddy old Thames, and her patient was a disconcertingly silent man with a very elegantly cut suit and well manicured hands who was, she knew, staring at her bent head as she worked. She straightened her back as she finished and stood looking down at her handiwork, at the neatly curving row of seven stitches.

"Hmmph!" she grunted softly. "That'll heal very nicely, as long as you don't go slashing away at any more glasses. I'll give you some antibiotic powder on it to be on the safe side and a firm dressing. You'll please not go using it too much now – no soaking it in water or whatever. You'll have to get someone else to shave you and wash you, I daresay – but I've no doubt someone can arrange that – " she smiled at him then. "They certainly seem willing to arrange things very well, don't they?"

"Do they? Who are *they*?"

"The management! I've the distinct impression that nothing's too much trouble for them! Are you not comfortable here yourself?" she began to apply a bandage with swift neat turns of her wrist.

"Oh, very comfortable. I'm glad to find you have so

high an opinion of the Cadiz. Now we must wait and see if the Cadiz will have as high an opinion of you."

"Indeed we must!" she said sharply, a little nettled. "I hope *you* are reasonably satisfied with the treatment you've had!"

"Oh, indeed I'm reasonably satisfied!" he said, pulling his shirt cuff down and flicking a scrap of lint from it with a fastidious gesture.

He stood up then, and looked at her with the same unsmiling consideration, and then sketched a faint bow, which was so supercilious in its lightness that she found herself reddening with embarrassment.

"Good afternoon, señorita, and – Gracias."

"You are very welcome, Señor," she said, and knew her voice was crackling with dislike and didn't care. How dared he be so offhand with her! Irritation seethed under the surface as she stared at him and he stared back with his silky eyebrows slightly raised. "You will please return tomorrow morning for fresh dressings, and each day thereafter until I can remove the stitches in five days' time. Good afternoon to *you*!"

He turned and went to the door, and he had his hand on the knob before she remembered, and annoyed with herself, had to call him back.

"Señor! I'll need to keep a record of your care. Would you tell me your name and room number, if you please."

Moving quickly, with her head held high, she swept into her small office and returned with a pen and the record book in her hands, and he was still standing at the open door when she came back.

"My name? Sebastian Garcia, Señorita Cameron. My room number I think you will not require. Good afternoon," and he turned and went, closing the door softly behind him and leaving her standing with her cheeks scarlet with a mixture of embarrassment and anger.

4

At seven thirty, as the light in the sky over the Bay began to thicken a little and a chill air came to curl the leaves on the potted plants on the balconies, the phone on her desk shrilled and she jumped so much that her hand shook a little as she answered it.

"Hello? er – Digame?"

"Señorita Cameron?" the voice at the other end was breathless and soft and she had to strain a little to hear it. "This is Consuelo – I am the secretary of Señor Garcia. I have for you some messages and information. I am to ask you to come to the office of Señor Garcia to collect it. But I bring it to you if you prefer."

"Not at all," Isabel said crisply. "I am only too happy to obey Señor Garcia's calls! Where is the office?"

"It is on the main foyer floor, to the far side. The door is a mirror, but the desk porter will show you. Gracias, Señorita!"

She locked all the cabinets in the surgical room with great care, and after a moment's thought locked the outer door of the clinic too, tucking the keys into her belt again with a slightly malicious satisfaction; he wouldn't be able to go prowling around *her* surgery while she was responsible for it, managing director or not! And then realized how silly she was being, for there were almost certainly additional sets of keys for every part of the hotel.

37

The foyer was busy when she reached it, with several guests lounging about and chattering, and there were groups of them sitting hunched over card tables set up by the windows, from which the blue curtains were now drawn to show a clear view of the Bay and the far shore on which a few lights were beginning to wink and sparkle.

Some of the people stared at her with a coolly arrogant curiosity which far from embarrassing her, as she might have expected it to, had the effect of putting her on her mettle and she walked quickly across the marble floor, very aware of the crisp look of her uniform and her pretty cap, and grateful to the little shop assistant who had insisted she buy white tights and shoes for she knew they showed off her long legs to advantage. "They may be rich, these people," she thought "but I'm as good as they any day!" and then amused at this very Scottish piece of independent thinking relaxed enough to smile widely at a small child who came skittering across the floor to stare up at her in frank curiosity.

"Who are you?" he demanded in a high clear treble that made several of the card players look up in annoyance.

"I'm Sister Cameron. And who are *you*?"

"My name's Fred. I'm an actor astronaut and I'm going to have a kangaroo farm in Australia when I'm not going to the moon."

"Fred? That is a remarkably interesting name for someone like you. You look like a Fred," Isabel said gravely. "And the best sort of actor astronaut kangaroo farmers are always called Fred."

He beamed at her, a huge smile that revealed a large gap in his front teeth. "I thought you looked sensible. Not like *her*!" He jerked his head sideways and she followed his indication to see a fragile looking girl with very fair hair falling in a great sheet over her shoulders and wearing a slender well-fitting leopard-skin patterned catsuit. She was

38

talking very animatedly to the man beside her; a square set grey-headed man with a cigar firmly clamped between his teeth and his eyes half closed against the clouds of smoke he was emitting. The girl turned her head to look about her as Isabel saw her, clearly searching for somebody.

"She thinks my name's Daniel," Fred said disgustedly.

"Danny!" the girl had a soft voice but it reached clearly across the crowded foyer. "Come here, darling – it's time for bed soon – "

"See what I mean?" the child said with even more disgust in his voice. "Danny! When anyone could *see* I'm a Fred! Mothers!" and he slouched away across the floor, presenting a back view of short denim trousers that had parted company at the waist from the vivid yellow shirt he wore, and socks that were so wrinkled over his ankles that his shoes were almost invisible. Isabel caught the fair girl's eye and smiled but she seemed not to notice and turned back to chatter again to the man beside her, apparently quite forgetting that she had mentioned the child's bedtime.

Isabel found the office without too much difficulty though its door was neatly hidden as part of a wall of mirrors. Consuelo proved to be a statuesque girl with dark hair worn in classic Spanish fashion in wings over each temple, and a knot at the nape of the neck, but a friendly manner that had nothing of the equally classic Spanish haughtiness about it.

"How is life in London now?" she asked eagerly. "I miss it so much – Carnaby Street, and the Kings Road and all the wonderful life – I was au pair for two years you know? In Hampstead. I was very happy – "

The messages that she had to deliver, once she stopped – reluctantly – her chatter about the London she remembered, were detailed and specific.

"Señor Garcia says first he has no further need to

arrange a special meeting with you. You will understand, he says, why this is so," Consuelo cocked an eye at her. "The injury – this was your doing, hmm?"

"Not the injury," Isabel said dryly. "Just the repair of it."

"Ha – perdone – of course – but you knew I meant that, yes?"

"I knew," Isabel smiled. "Not to worry. So no further need for a meeting! Well, I'll have to see him every day for a few days, whether he likes it or no, and that's all about it!"

Consuelo smiled too. "If he doesn't like it, he doesn't come. It is clear you do not yet understand our Señor Garcia. He is a very – strong – man. Hmm?"

"And I'm no' precisely a softie mysel'," Isabel said sharply and then stopped. When the accent of her childhood suddenly made itself as clear as that it meant that she was more bothered than she knew, and she was surprised at herself. But then she relaxed a little. She had been anxious about meeting her new boss anyway, there had been a hectic day behind her, what with the journey and her arrival and all that emotional upheaval, and to have to stitch a nasty wound in a hurry only to find that her patient was the boss she had been so nervous about meeting – it was no wonder the whole business had got under her skin so much. She'd really have to learn to be a little less edgy, she told herself.

"And here is a detailed list of your daily duties. I typed it very quickly – I hope it is all understandable for you?" Consuelo said anxiously.

"Oh, it's fine, just fine," Isabel said, a little abstractedly for she was reading it carefully. Her day was to start at eight-thirty sharp, with her attendance at the clinic until one. Thereafter she was free until four p.m. unless special calls were made upon her in emergencies. She would hold another clinic session until six-thirty, and was then free again, unless there were emergencies. As part of her clinic sessions she was to see the staff, those who were ill and those who were in need of special treatment recommended by their doctors, but which could be done during working hours. She was to wear her uniform only during clinic sessions, and never after seven-thirty at night, certainly, for Señor Garcia wished always to see such members of the staff as used the hotel's public rooms looking as well dressed as befitted the quality of the establishment.

This particular phrase first made Isabel snort with amusement at its pomposity and then rapidly review in her mind's eye the clothes she had brought with her. There were two or three suitable outfits, but clearly she'd have to spend some of her first salary cheque on a few more. "If I want to use the public rooms, that is," she said aloud a little sharply.

"If you – you do not wish to use the hotel in the evenings? What then will you do, Señorita? The Cadiz, it is one of the most fashionable hotels in Palma, in all the Island, indeed! It is a privilege that Señor Garcia gives his top staff, that we can sit in the bar and the lounges, and talk with such guests as wish to talk, and to dance and swim in the pool! There are no other hotel owners I know of who do such for their senior staff. This is why so many people they want to work here! Always we have the best staff, the most superb of everybody, because it is so good to work here!"

Consuelo looked really upset, and Isabel touched her hand and smiled at her. It wasn't fair to vent some of her own irritation with the supercilious man she was working for on this girl who also worked for him, and patently liked him very much. Isabel thought with a sudden insight – he can't be that bad if his secretary is so attached to him.

"Of course I appreciate the chance to use the hotel as

41

though I were a guest – and thank you for typing it all so nicely for me," she looked down at the papers in her hand. "Is that all?"

"There is another page," Consuelo said, and showed her, and Isabel read on. On Sundays there were to be no clinics; only if there were emergencies would she be needed but on Saturdays she was to remain in the clinic throughout the midday break, since many guests departed and others arrived on this day, and she would be needed to care for those who had been in any way disturbed by the journey, or who required medicines before embarking on their journey home.

She had to admit that the duties were far from arduous, and that considerable thought had gone into making her work as easy as possible; the equipment provided in the clinic showed that. But there was a chilliness about the wording of the paper in her hands, and impulsively she said: "Did Señor Garcia write this himself, Consuelo? I mean, did he tell you what to say, and let you put it in your own words?"

"Oh, no," Consuelo was shocked, "Of course he dictated it! For Señor Garcia you do not alter one word, one comma! It is well done, yes? He speaks so many languages, and all with such perfection!" She shook her head and grimaced her admiration. "It is very remarkable."

"Very," Isabel said. "Well, I suppose since it's gone six-thirty I must change, or this remarkable man will be after me for breaking one of the Rules of the Establishment."

"He would not be pleased if you were still in your uniform at dinner," Consuelo agreed, clearly not aware of the note of sarcasm in Isabel's voice. "He takes his dinner early – at eight-thirty, but you have time to change before he comes down, so do not worry."

"I'm not worrying," Isabel said, turning to go. "Must *I* have dinner at eight-thirty?"

"Oh, no, you can come to the dining-room at any time up to ten o'clock. Here in Spain we keep much later hours than you do in England. It is the hot sun of summer, you understand! Not until dark can any of us face the big meal. So, I must now return to my home. For me, I stay in the hotel only in the evenings on Saturday and Sunday," she sounded a little mournful. "Los padres – my parents, you understand? They say I must go out only on these days, so at home I must be in each evening."

Isabel stopped at the door. "How old are you, Consuelo?"

"How old? I am twenty-four, Señorita Cameron."

"Then you're old enough, surely, to decide how you will spend your evenings? I mean, you aren't a baby – you're a grown-up person – "

Consuelo looked startled. "But I must do as my parents say."

"Why?"

"Why? I – I – " Consuelo floundered. "They are my parents! Of course I must do as they say! Here in Spain we are not as the English, you know!" there was a hint of pride in her voice. "We do not permit the young people to tell the parents what to do, as in England!"

"I'm sorry – of course, I forgot. This is Spain, and I had no right. Forgive me. You just sounded so fed up – "

"Fed up?"

"Miserable. Sad, you know?"

Consuelo smiled then, a little ruefully. "I remember the word. You are right, of course. I am sometimes annoyed that I stay at home on all the good evenings. When I was au pair in England – well, I must not talk of that, it makes me – how is it said – discontent. And it is not so bad! There is Tomas – " she smiled widely. "Mi caballero – my boyfriend, you know? It is not so bad – "

Isabel dressed for the evening with rather more care than she was prepared to admit. She had no intention

43

of going in to dinner until long after Señor Garcia would have left the restaurant, and she certainly had no intention of seeking his company during the course of the evening. But all the same –

So she bathed and dressed in the soft green silk dress she had bought to wear at the Consultants' Dinner with Jason a few months ago – a memory that had to be very firmly pushed into its place – and brushed her hair until the coppery lights leapt out of it, and put on her makeup with very careful hands.

And found that when she was ready that it was still only eight-thirty and hunger was gnawing at her in no uncertain manner. She realized almost with surprise that apart from a breakfast of black coffee, the plastic snacks on the plane and the tea and biscuits of the afternoon she had had no solid food all day.

"So I'm away to my meal!" she told her reflection in the mirror. "And if Señor Snooty Garcia is still there in the restaurant it's no' my affair, is it? No, it is not, Isabel Cameron!"

At the entrance to the lift in the foyer she lingered for a moment, looking about her with a sudden shyness; she had been aware of the luxurious status of the hotel ever since she arrived, but now, quite suddenly, it was hurled at her and almost overwhelmed her.

There was a smell of richness in the air – expensive wine, expensive cigars, expensive perfume, expensive food, and if the guests she had seen in the restaurant at lunchtime had looked rich, they now looked positively millionairish. One of the women drifted by, talking busily to her silent companion in a white dinner jacket, and wearing a dress that Isabel could see at a glance had probably cost half of her own salary for a year; a full length confection of heavy dull grey satin with great bands of mink in the identical colour swathing the skirt, the neckline and the cuffs. A magnificent dress, and worn with an air of casual comfort that somehow made it seem even more costly.

And there were other splendid dresses, all as clearly expensive as each other, and for one brief moment Isabel wanted to turn tail and run back to her room, to pretend she was unwell and phone to ask Jaime Mendoza to arrange to have a meal sent up to her.

But her customary good sense moved in; she could hardly eat every meal in her room, hiding from the guests, and anyway why should she? She was staff, after all, not pretending to be anything that she wasn't; so she lifted her chin in the characteristic way she did when she had made a decision, and walked across the great marble expanse to the double doors at the end.

She lingered for a moment at the door, looking at the tables filled with chattering people, at the waiters skimming about at great speed with terrifyingly high piles of plates with gleaming metal covers on them, and trays filled with glasses and bottles. At one side of the entrance was a table which was so incredibly like a picture in a travel brochure that she wanted to laugh aloud, but its very realness made her laughter shrivel. Great red lobsters jostled with baskets of more delicate pink prawns, all long antennae and curly tails, while on one side a ham sat surrounded by a multitude of different shaped and sized sausages, and on the other a bewildering array of cheeses spread itself over a green-leaf-bedecked wooden board. And between all were heaps of artichokes and avocados, asparagus and apples, tomatoes and oranges and thick skinned lemons and red and green and yellow peppers – there was so much of it that it almost took her appetite away.

"Señorita? You are the new nurse, yes? I am Felipe, head waiter, and I take you to your table."

"How do you do, Felipe?" Isabel said, and held out her

hand and after a moment he took it and they shook a little solemnly, and then he turned and led the way through the restaurant to the table at the far side, the one she and Jaime had used at tea time.

But there was no-one at it now, and she sat down in the chair that Felipe held for her with great punctiliousness, and unwrapping her napkin and spreading it on her knee, looked swiftly round beneath her lashes. There was no sign anywhere of Señor Garcia, and she breathed a soft sigh of relief and straightened up a little to look about her more comfortably.

Felipe, looking very fatherly with his heavy shape and grizzled head moved about the restaurant with such elegance and speed that he seemed to be everywhere at once; he watched his waiters like a hawk, and it was amusing to see how he pounced on the most minor of errors of behaviour in the young men who bustled so busily from the leather-covered doors that swung hectically between the kitchen and the restaurant, and their allotted tables.

She read the menu with a sense of bewilderment at first, and then found the English translation and settled down to enjoy herself. However Calvinist her upbringing, Isabel had a healthy respect for her stomach and a decided taste for good food and wine that a year as Jason's girl had developed, for Jason, whatever else he was, was a man who knew what was good, and was determined to have it.

So she ate gazpacho, that icily cold pepper and garlic flavoured Andalucian soup, and a small dish of paella with its yellow saffron flavoured rice with pieces of chicken and lamb and mussels and prawns plentifully mixed with it, and then cold chicken and salad, and enjoyed it all enormously. It was excellent food, excellently cooked, and served in just the right quantities – enough to enjoy

46

each dish, but not so much that she was tempted to over-eat.

She sat back in her seat, waiting for Carlos, the waiter who was looking after her (and she had immediately asked the name of the boy who was assigned to her table, and made a point of using it, remembering how much she herself hated the anonymity of being called "Sister" and appreciated the charm of people who took the trouble to use her name) to bring her the fresh orange she had chosen to end her meal. And was startled when he did arrive, for he was carrying a glass of champagne on the small tray as well as her orange.

"What's this?" she asked as he put the glass in front of her, and then skilfully began to peel her orange, first impaling it on a long slender fork. "I didn't ask for anything to drink!"

"Señor Garcia, Señorita," Carlos said. "He say, to welcome a new member of staff to the Cadiz – he is a good boss, hey?" and he grinned at her cheerfully, and began to slice the orange very thinly with his murderously long thin knife.

She looked about her again, and this time she saw him, sitting across the great restaurant on the far side, and he was looking at her very directly.

For a moment she wanted to pretend she hadn't noticed his gaze, and then castigated herself for being so ungracious; the man may have been disagreeable before, when they met in the clinic, but he was now clearly trying to be pleasant. So she picked up the glass and raised it a little in his direction before sipping it, and he inclined his head very slightly, and then looked away; and not in any way did his facial expression change.

"Damned icicle," she muttered, and Carlos said "Perdone?" and she shook her head, and smiled at him and thanked him for his efforts with the orange.

It was almost quarter to ten by the time she had finished her fruit and her wine, and she stood up to leave the restaurant feeling decidedly better than she had, but quite extraordinarily tired. Her eyelids were heavy and she could feel a constant desire to yawn lurking behind her jawbones, and knew she had eaten too well altogether, and that the glass of champagne had added to the general effect.

Señor Garcia's table was empty, she noticed, and she left the restaurant obscurely glad of it; with luck she wouldn't have to see him to thank him for the champagne until the next day, when she would be in the clinic in her uniform, and thus somehow protected; in uniform, when she could be every inch the Sister, strict, cool and remote, it would be easy to deal with his irritating manner; but now, lulled half asleep with food and wine vulnerable in green silk, she couldn't face him.

But even as she told herself this, crossing the long corridor towards the lounges where she could hear the soft sound of music and the chatter of many voices, Señor Garcia appeared from one of the doors at the side, and came across towards her, as unsmiling as ever.

"Señorita Cameron, good evening. I hope you found your dinner good, and that you are comfortable still at the Cadiz?"

"Thank you, it was very good – and I am very comfortable. And er – I'm to thank you for the champagne. It was a – very good of you." She knew she sounded flustered and was angry with herself for it. Damn it, there was nothing to be flustered about!

He made that supercilious little bow again, and she frowned a little, and then he said in the same even and rather flat tone. "This is your first visit to Palma di Mallorca?"

"Yes. I've never been anywhere in Spain before."

"Then you will permit me to offer my car for your use, should you wish to see the city, and some of the nearby interesting sights. My chauffeur is outside and ready when you are."

She went very red, and then white, and opened her mouth and closed it again, silently, for all the world like a gawky schoolgirl. After the things she had been thinking about this man, to be asked out by him in this way – it was almost more than she could take in.

She opened her mouth again, but this time she was interrupted before she could say anything, and she whirled in stunned surprise at the sound of her name.

"Isabel? Er, Miss Cameron? – remember me?"

It was Biff, standing there with a panama hat held in one broad brown hand and his nice brown face split with a very white smile, and she smiled back at him with unfeigned delight. At least she didn't have to say anything to Señor Garcia while Biff was here.

"Well, hello!" she said with great warmth in her voice. "Er – may I introduce – er Señor Garcia – my – er – employer. Mr. Squires – "

"Glad to know you, Señor," Biff said, holding out his hand. "Hey, that's a nasty looking bandage you have there! Has he put you to work already, Isabel? Well, well! – "

"A small accident, no more," Señor Garcia said. "How do you do, Señor Squires."

"I don't know if Miss Cameron here is free or not – I was kind of hoping I'd be able to take her round the town and show her a few things. Can you spare her, do you think, Señor Garcia!"

"Oh, no!" Isabel started to laugh. "Oh, this is too much! First Señor Garcia offers to take me to see the town, and now you! It's too much altogether! What do I do? Toss up? I feel like a rope in a tug of war!"

49

She knew she was chattering absurdly, and giggling like a great baby, but the combined effects of tiredness, a big dinner and the second glass of champagne in one day were enough to make the most taciturn of individuals into a garrulous one – or so her secret little voice whispered to her, as she looked almost hopelessly from one man to the other.

"My offer was to lend you my car and the services of my chauffeur, Señorita, so there is, you see, no need to make any difficult choices. No doubt Mr. Squires will be as happy to escort you in my car as in a taxi. Buenas noches, Señor, Señorita – " and with yet another of those chilly inclinations of the head he turned and went across the foyer towards his mirror-doored office, leaving Isabel with her hand held to her flaming cheeks, and Biff Squires staring after him in puzzlement.

5

She came down to breakfast at seven-thirty, walking out of her room and going down in the lift under the curious stares of the small army of white-aproned and capped chambermaids who seemed to be swarming everywhere, with dusters and brooms and buckets akimbo. But there were no guests in the restaurant and for that she was grateful. Last night, after she had escaped to her room from the agonizing embarrassment of the episode in the lobby, she had sworn that she would go straight back to England. Even staying at the Royal and seeing Jason every day wouldn't be as ghastly as all this.

But this morning she had gone out on to her balcony and stared down at the gardens, at the overalled men bustling about the plant borders and arranging the loungers and skimming the swimming pools of dust and floating leaves, had smelled the exciting freshness of the new day, seen the sun lifting the bay into creases of diamond edged sapphire loveliness, and had an attack of stubbornness. So she had made a fool of herself! So what about it? To go scuttling back to London like a daft bairn would be to make herself even more of a fool. She'd stay put, and Señor Full-of-Himself Sebastian Garcia could go to blazes.

Carlos was ready and waiting for her, busily arranging a few tables out on the restaurant balcony, though the rest of the tables in the big room were clearly set for lunch. She settled herself under the awning as he pulled a chair out for her.

"Don't many people come to breakfast?" she asked.

"Ah, no, Señorita – they like to eat in their rooms, these guests. Soon the waiters are running everywhere with trays – it is a busy time! But me, today, I have the restaurant and it is easy for me!" His face split into a great grin. "So, for you – you want the big English breakfast, si?"

She thought of porridge and bacon and eggs and looked at the row of palms that edged the balcony and the way their needle leaves were etched against the vivid blue of the sky, and shook her head firmly.

"Certainly not, Carlos! In Spain, I eat as the Spaniards do! I can eat porridge any time – so just bring me what you think is best."

He nodded in great approval and hurried away, and she sat with her chin propped on her hands staring out at the morning and felt her heart lift. It was a beautiful place to be, and there was a whole summer ahead of her, and as for last night – after a moment she began to smile. It *was* funny, after all. Less than twenty four hours after leaving a broken heart behind her in grimy old London, she was seeing herself as the sort of girl men almost fought over – too ridiculous for words.

And there's another thing, she thought then, as Carlos came towards her from the kitchen doors bearing a tray in his hands; "I've only thought of Jason once or twice since I got here, after weeks of having him in my mind constantly, almost like a sore tooth." If the object of this Spanish exercise was to rid herself of his lingering ghost, she was clearly going to achieve it.

"Now, Señorita Cameron!" Carlos said. "Try this!" He put in front of her a goblet that was filled with a deep orangy yellow liquid, the outside dewed with moisture,

52

and she sipped it and let the taste slide over her tongue and shivered with pleasure.

"It is juice, fresh juice I just squeeze for you myself – orange and the little – you call them tangerines, yes? And grapefruit and some lemon juice and a *leetle* sugar. Bueno, si?"

"Mucho bueno!"

"And also, I bring you café con leche – coffee with hot milk, the rolls, and these – these are very special – typico – typical of the Island."

He uncovered a little cane basket, and showed her a couple of big flat curly cakes, dusted with sugar and gleaming a delectable golden brown in the sunlight, "These are ensaimadas – you taste, you see – with the mermelada de naranja – the marmalade – "

Obediently she took one of the cakes and pulled off a piece and spread it with a little of the marmalade he gave her, and then nodded, her mouth full, for they tasted as delicious as they looked. And Carlos grinned at her, and poured a cup of coffee for her, and went away to leave her in the clear light of the Mediterranean morning to enjoy her meal.

She was whistling softly beneath her breath as she made her way down through the foyer to the floor where her clinic was, full of breakfast energy. The maids nodded and murmured "Buenos dias!" as she went by, and she cried "Buenos dias" back, childishly pleased with her ability to say so simple a Spanish phrase. There was a maid waiting to get into her clinic, too, when she got there, and as soon as Isabel had unlocked she set to work to swab the already gleaming terrazzo floor, and to polish the chrome to blinding perfection.

After a little thought, Isabel prepared a tray of sterile instruments and dressings, ready for what might come in the way of work. There was no way of knowing how many

53

people would need attention – no way of knowing if there would be any at all for that matter, but she knew there would be at least one, and she certainly had no intention of being caught unprepared by him.

She had just finished the tray and had set the trolley as ready as she could when the desk telephone rang.

"Good morning!" a little voice clacked in response to her cheerful "Digame". "I thought you'd be pretty miserable this morning, but you sound great! I mean, after last night – you looked pretty sick – "

"Good morning, Biff. No, I'm fine. I was a bit tired last night, I admit, and I'm sorry I shot off like that. It was really very kind of you to have come to see me, and to ask me to go out, and I owe you an apology. I really behaved very childishly."

"The hell with that!" the little voice said indignantly. "If anyone behaved badly it's that lousy sonofa – that guy you're working for. If I ever saw or heard a slob in action, it's that piece of – of – "

"Hey, Biff!" Isabel said, amused. "There's no need to be so very annoyed with him! I can't pretend I'm exactly his greatest admirer this morning, but all the same, I did make a fool of myself. The man offered me the use of his car and I was daft enough to think – well, I was tired, and one way and another – "

"Listen, honey, I don't care if you *did* make a mistake – which frankly I doubt. I mean, I reckon the guy *did* ask you out and got hit in the eye when I turned up and got back at you real vicious – but what I mean is, even if he *did* only offer you his lousy car and lousier chauffeur, if he'd been any kind of a real man he'd not have behaved like – I mean, in his shoes, I'd never have said anything so lousy! I'd have said – this is my date, and you go play in someone else's yard – and I'd have taken you off around the town and given you a real good time – "

"I'm sure you would, Biff. And thank you. You really are very kind, and very nice, and already I feel much better about it all. Really, I've been very lucky! Yesterday you talked me out of my flying nerves, and this morning you smooth my ruffled feathers! Not that they're ruffled, I assure you. I'd got over the whole thing anyway. I've usually more sense than to get myself into a great state over sillinesses! But thanks for the thought – and thanks for phoning so early! I had to get up at seven, because I have to start clinic at eight thirty, but you didn't have to!"

He chuckled richly. "Indeed I did! I'm a working type too, remember! Today I have to go over to Andraitx to see about a site there. But look, Isabel – can it be Isabel now, by the way? Or shall I stick with Miss Cameron?"

She laughed too, "Isabel, of course."

"Okay, Isabel. Listen, what time are you free today? Apart from midday, I mean. This whole damned Island grinds to a halt from one till four – tonight is what I'm asking about."

"I finish at seven thirty," she said. "But – "

"No buts. This time I don't get done in the eye. Tonight you're *my* date – okay? We'll eat someplace interesting, and maybe we'll get to see some Flamenco. I'll pick you up there at around eight. Can you be ready?"

"Thank you, Biff. I can be ready; and I'll look forward to it."

"That'll show him!" she thought obscurely as she hung up. And knew she was being ridiculous, for how could it? She would hardly be likely to march up to him and say "I'm going out with Biff tonight, so Yah sucks, boo!" would she? Really, she was getting positively paranoid about this man Garcia. He piqued her, and hurt her sense of amour propre, that's what it was, she told herself. Rather like when a new surgeon came to the Royal, and tried to impose his will on her. She had always made it clear that her theatres were run her way, and that she was at least the equal of the men who worked there. No one was going to make sturdy, independent Sister Cameron into a mere lackey, a handmaiden of Aesculapius, and everyone might as well know it.

She looked at her watch, annoyed with herself for letting her thoughts run away with her so. Eight forty, and no sign of any patients. For a moment she felt real anxiety. Suppose there turned out to be hardly any patients ever? After all, a hotel wasn't like a hospital with something always going on in the illness field! Maybe she'd have nothing to do apart from dealing with the odd cuts and bruises; the summer suddenly seemed to yawn in front of her, workless, empty and interminable.

She hurried to the door, planning on going up to the foyer to ask Jaime Mendoza whether everyone knew she was on duty, ready to start work, and stopped short as she reached the little waiting room.

It was quite full, with several people leaning against the walls and sharing the available chairs, and beyond them she could see several more in the corridor outside. And she smiled broadly, a smile of pure relief, and said "Good morning – ah – Buenos Dias!" and there was a soft chorus of response.

They were all staff, every one of them, and they filed in in order, to present her with assorted bumps and bruises and half healed cuts and grazes. As she treated each one, carefully noting names and departments – kitchens, gardens, boiler rooms – she knew she was under surveillance. Clearly the word had gone out and everyone who could was coming to see the new enfermera, to assess her capabilities and decide whether or not they would patronize her clinic again.

There was a lull in the demand for her care at around

ten, as she sent off, suitably bandaged, the last of the patients who had arrived with the eight thirty rush, and then, half an hour later, another batch of staff arrived and she breathed a sigh of real relief. Clearly, she *was* approved; her first patients had gone back to their departments and reported favourably, and sent their friends and colleagues along. And from ten thirty until almost twelve thirty she dealt with a steady stream of patients, while learning a number of Spanish words she hadn't met before.

"Tiritas – " one chambermaid said, showing her a roll of sticky plaster, and "El unguento, por favor?" asked another showing her the rows of pots of ointments in one of the cabinets. She strapped a strained ankle, while the owner of it spelled out "El tobillo – " and lanced a boil in a finger and was told it was "El furunculo di dedo – " And when she repeated the words, her patients nodded and beamed their approval, and altogether made her feel she was doing very well.

At a quarter to one, she telephoned Jaime Mendoza, who was so full of chatter that she could hardly get a word in edgeways; but at length she managed to explain what she wanted.

"I don't suppose I'll be so busy every day," she said. "This morning all the staff wanted to have a look at the clinic, I think. But I don't want to keep the waiting room full of people all the time – "

"Oh, no, certainly not – this is bad, I agree very bad," Jaime said fussily. "When they should be working it is not good they come and sit and waste your time, no?"

"Oh, for heaven's sake, I'm not complaining about that!" Isabel said hastily. "Though I realize I'll not be too popular with some of the senior people if half their staff are hanging round my clinic most of the morning! I just didn't want the waiting room crowded because it's so uncomfortable for them. It's not designed to hold more than half a dozen folk, after all! So would you send a notice round asking people to make appointments when things aren't urgent? If they phone me here in the afternoons I can fix an appointment for the next day, you see."

"But of course – an idea of great sense, that. I arrange it at once. Now, Isabella, it is nearly time for el almuerzo – for lunch, yes? And if you will come to the desk on your way up, I am happy if you go in with me. I wait for you in ten minutes, si?"

She tidied the clinic and put the instruments in the sterilizer ready for the afternoon, and locked up carefully before going up to meet Jaime Mendoza. "I'll have to make it clear I don't want to take lunch with him every day," she thought, as she made her way up through the hotel to the foyer. "Quite apart from the fact that he needs discouraging, I'd be bored out of mind – "

But once more, she need not have worried. When Jaime led her into the restaurant, bustling in front of her and delivering scolding remarks on all sides as they passed less exalted members of the staff than themselves, she found that a double table had been set in the place she had sat at for tea and dinner the day before.

"At lunch, all the staff members that use the restaurant sit together, you see? This way we are a team, verdad?"

He sat himself at the head of the table, after carefully leading Isabel to the seat on his right, and beaming round at the group, introduced her.

"Señorita Cameron, here is Señora Lupez, our house-keeper."

A heavy woman of about forty five, wearing a severe black dress that didn't at all suit a very round smiling face, nodded at her.

"Consuelo – ah, you have met, yes?" Consuelo and Isabel smiled at each other. "Ricardo Fernandez, who

58

is our – the man who looks after the money, the books, you understand – "

"Accountant?" said Isabel.

"Ah, of course – accountant – " Jaime said, and Señor Fernandez bobbed his narrow head, and returned his attention to the roll and butter he was eating. "And here also is Pepe Delgado, who is our – er – "

"I am the public relations, Mees Cameron." Pepe was a small neatly dressed and rather round faced boy – and Isabel saw him at once as a boy rather than a man even though he was clearly a year or two older than herself; there was something very fresh and eager about him. "And I speak, of course, considerable English, so you have problems I am happy to – "

"There will be no need," Jaime said a little grandly. "I am here for this purpose. Now, we eat, si? Carlos, you bring to us the wine at once, and then we start with the meal."

She enjoyed it all; the chatter of the other people at the table, even Jaime's constant flow of talk giving her pleasure, and the good food and the fruit juice she chose instead of wine. The others were amused at her English refusal to drink wine in the middle of a working day, and Pepe assured her solemnly that before she returned to " – that cold island of the North" that she would be accustomed to filling her veins with the "sunshine from a bottle" that was Spanish wine. "He must be good at his job" Isabel thought with a spark of amusement, "He even talks like an advertisement – "

Lunch over, Consuelo suggested that they go together to swim in the pool, and Isabel delightedly agreed. She collected her swimsuit from her room and met Consuelo in the foyer at two o'clock.

"Perhaps I show you more of the hotel before we swim?" Consuelo suggested. "Or have you seen all?"

Isabel said she would love to see the rest of the hotel and had certainly not seen all, and spent half an hour following Consuelo from one splendid and charming room to another. There were card rooms and games rooms, and writing rooms and television rooms; and a hairdresser's shop and bookshop and delightful little boutiques on the floor two levels below the one where her clinic was.

"It is because we are built on the side of the cliff, you see?" Consuelo explained. "The street level at the front is four above the lowest floor we have – and then we have two more terraces below. It is very beautiful, yes?"

"Very," Isabel said, a little weakly.

"We are lucky to work here, yes?" Consuelo went on happily. "So good a hotel, so kind a man to work for – I am very happy. He owns all this, and is still so good to his staff – " she waved an expressive hand around the room they were in, a wide lounge with a wooden floor – unusual where nearly every floor was of marble – and an elegantly fitted bar curving along one side. "You like this room? It is for the dancing – every night, when the summer is here, we open this wall – you see? It is all shutters – and then the room is open to the sea and the sky, and we have music, and we dance and it is very, very beautiful."

"Very beautiful," Isabel said, and then added a little sharply, "You make so much fuss about your Señor Garcia – he sounds more like a saint than an ordinary man. Personally, I don't find him all that marvellous – " and then could have bitten her tongue off, for Consuelo looked so upset.

"But he is of the kindest, I promise you!" she cried. "Why do you say this?"

"Ach, I'm sorry, Consuelo. Take no notice," Isabel said. "It's just that he never seems to smile or be – well, ordinarily friendly! Never says a word more than he must."

60

"You prefer Jaime Mendoza?" Consuelo said, looking out of the corner of her eyes at Isabel, and Isabel laughed and said, "Heavens, no! He never *stops* talking! Maybe you're right at that." And they both laughed, and went off together to swim in the pool in good humour with each other.

There was no one there but themselves for the first half hour or so, and they stretched themselves out luxuriously on the long mattresses and dozed a little in the sun. Isabel could feel it stroking her skin, as she lay there with her arms thrown out and her eyes closed, and let it creep into her muscles, softening them into relaxation and peace. "A great life, this," she thought sleepily. "I could really develop quite a taste for it – "

"Well, there you are! I've been calling all over the hotel for you!"

Isabel opened her eyes, and blinked into the sun, and then screwing her lids against the brightness squinted upwards. Mrs. Connaught was standing above her, looking down with a cool stare that seemed to take in Isabel's simple black swimsuit and compare it very unfavourably with the white suede one she was herself wearing.

Isabel sat up, and reached for her towelling robe. "I'm sorry. I didn't know I was wanted. I was in my clinic until one, of course. You could have found me there if you'd come down."

"I'm not about to come to any clinic, thank you! Not when all the kitchen maids and porters are cluttering the place, as I understand they were this morning!"

"Cluttering?" Isabel was standing now, and tied the girdle of her robe with a sharp tug. "Nobody was cluttering anything. I only had *patients* there. And only for as long as was necessary for their care. I assure you you wouldn't have had to wait for very long."

"I'm not interested in waiting at all!" Mrs. Connaught

said. "You will come to my room this afternoon at four thirty, and deal with the matter then."

"I'm sorry, Mrs. Connaught," Isabel said, and her face was white with controlled anger. "At four thirty I must be in the clinic. My instructions are to remain there to look after any person who comes needing my care, although of course I will see people in their rooms in an emergency. Do you have an emergency, Mrs. Connaught?"

The woman had turned away, but now she looked round and came back. Isabel was suddenly aware of three or four other guests sitting about on the swimming pool terrace, of Consuelo's anxious white face staring up at them both from her mattress and felt a twinge of fear. After all, this wasn't a hospital but an hotel, and maybe the guests *did* have a right to treat her like any other member of the staff. But then she saw the sneer curled round Mrs. Connaught's lips and firmed her own. To hell with her! She was not going to be bullied by such a one!

"That's for me to decide, isn't it?" Mrs. Connaught said coldly. "If I call you and say I want to see you in my room, then I want to see you in my room. So, be there at four thirty, d'you understand?" and she marched away towards the bar, her white clad hips swinging above her sunbrowned legs, leaving Isabel standing staring after her with her mouth set mulishly.

"Oh, Isabel, I hope you will go, yes?" Consuelo said anxiously. "I know she is a very hard woman – everyone says she is very hard, but – she is the friend of Señor Garcia, and there is always trouble if she is upset. You will go to her at four thirty?"

Isabel bent to pick up her beach bag. "Go to her?" she said in a clear voice that could be heard across the whole terrace. "Go to her? I'm damned if I do. And she *and* Señor Garcia can do what they like about it!"

6

As the clock crept round from four to four fifteen her intent was high. She was not going to go to Vanda Connaught's room to deal with whatever imagined ill the woman had, and that was all about it.

But as four fifteen became four twenty and then four twentyfive her resolve wavered a little. After all, what was she here for? She was being highly paid and comfortably maintained in exchange for providing medical services for the hotel's guests and staff. To expect from guests who were paying big bills the sort of politeness and appreciation that English patients offered in English hospitals – with their long tradition of Lady Bountiful charitableness that demanded grovelling gratitude – was hardly justified. And, what was more, a rather unpleasant sidelight on her own attitudes, she told herself sternly.

But then she remembered the cool and calculated insolence of the woman's tone, the deliberate attempt to belittle her in others' eyes, and hardened her resolve again. Her objection was not to going to the woman to treat her tuppeny ha'penny complaint or whatever it was, but to being spoken to so abominably. She would *not* go, and she snapped the lid of the sterilizer closed over the forceps she had used on the single patient from the gardening staff who had come to her afternoon clinic session and began to plan in her mind exactly what she would say to Señor Garcia about his precious guest.

Certainly a plan was needed, she thought. He'd be turning up shortly for his own dressing, surely, and she wanted to be ready for him.

The phone rang sharply on her desk and she hurried across to answer it.

"Señorita Enfermera – si? Señorita – oiga? – Señorita?" a voice gabbled as she picked it up.

"Si – what's the matter? – er – qué hay?"

At once the voice broke into a stream of excited Spanish, and she had to hold the phone away from her ear and shout to make herself heard.

"Haga el favor de hablar más despacio – please speak more *slowly*."

The voice gasped, stopped and then started again.

"Señorita – ha habido un accidente – entiende – "

"An accident – yes, I understand – where?"

"Pierde la sangre! – esta gravemente herido – "

"He's bleeding? It's a bad accident, you mean? Where? I'll come at once – "

" – echa sangre – "

"I understand! Someone's bleeding after an accident! But *where*?" she was shouting in her frustration. "Tell me where and I'll come!"

There was a clatter, and then someone else came on to the line. "Señorita Cameron? This is Felipe – the butcher has cut himself badly – we are in the kitchen, yes?"

"I'm on my way!" and she dropped the phone and reached for her bag of equipment, and almost ran from the clinic, but still found time to lock the outer door before she left, for her concern about the safety of the drugs there was not to be forgotten even in an emergency.

When she reached the kitchen, hurrying through the restaurant to the leather covered double doors, she found a scene of high excitement which would have done justice to a multiple car smash. Dozens of people seemed to be

64

milling about, and she had to push her way through a knot of chattering gesticulating waiters and kitchen maids to where she guessed her patient was waiting.

"Marchesé!" she called loudly, giving her voice all the authority she could. "Go away from here, all of you – marchesé!"

They fell back a little, and made way for her, and she found that they had been clustered round a big wooden table on which was lying a man in a white apron worn over a white canvas suit. But his apron wasn't entirely white; the front was splashed with an ominous crimson stain that spread right across it, and the face above was very pale, the eyes closed as the man breathed gaspingly and rapidly.

"He's lost a hell of a lot of blood," she thought at once, staring at him and automatically she reached for his pulse. "He's shocked and short of oxygen – " and she moved in closer rapidly undoing her case as she did so.

Felipe was holding the man's hand wrapped in a horribly red wet towel, and at once she took it from him and raised it high.

"Like this, Felipe – hold it high – it will help stop the bleeding a little – " she looked over her shoulder at the gaping faces which had closed in on her again. "Call an ambulance, one of you – haga mandar una ambulancia – rapido, rapido! And the rest of you, go *away* – marchesé, do you hear me? Tell them, Felipe – "

As Felipe spoke in sharp peremptory Spanish and one of the waiters went rushing to the telephone, she reached into the bag and pulled out a dressing and then leaned across to take the injured limb from Felipe, who relinquished his hold gratefully.

"I give him some brandy, yes?" he asked anxiously, for the man was beginning to moan a little, rolling his head about and gasping.

"No!" she said quickly. "Nothing. He must go to hospital fast, and they will treat him there. Brandy will make it difficult for them, and may make him worse – now, hold this – like that – well done – don't let go – " She had put a thick pad of dressing over the wound, and had blanched a little herself as she saw it, for the man had gashed his wrist and severed a main artery and the blood was pumping out horribly fast. Unless his blood loss stopped very soon he would be dead. And even as the thought came to her she knew that he wouldn't survive long enough to get to hospital. Something more drastic than the mere application of an emergency dressing would be needed here.

She bit her lip, and then reached again into her bag. She had added some items of her own to it, as soon as she had investigated its contents the evening before, and now she knew where everything was. The instruments were clean, but not sterile, but the chance of infection was a great deal less worrying than the chance the man would die.

So, moving as deliberately as she could, she took a pair of clipped artery forceps in one hand, and with the other carefully pulled back the dressing that Felipe had been holding in place.

"For God's sake don't move, man – " she said crisply. "If you can't look then close your eyes, but keep this hand still, you hear?"

Felipe was looking very white about the mouth, but he nodded as she pulled the last of the dressing away and the blood again began to spurt, Felipe turned his head to stare steadfastly at the wall on the other side of the kitchen.

It seemed to her that she was scrabbling with the point of her forceps for hours, and the blood slid over her own hands, making them slippery and awkward, but she swabbed away the flow and again reached for the bleeding point with her forceps. And almost praying she was right,

66

clipped them closely and mopped with the dressing at the raw wound.

And she had succeeded. As she mopped and no more blood came to fill the area with its terrifying crimson pool she knew she'd managed to find the severed end of the artery and clip it. Now, to find the other end and clip that, if it hadn't retracted into the wound –

She found it and clipped it, and then angling the forceps gently to one side to clear her view reached for a fresh dressing to clean the area properly. Now she could see it, a smallish wound, but sited so that the radial artery was cut right across.

"He'll be lucky not only to live but to keep his hand," she thought, as she strapped the forceps to the arm with a strip of plaster, leaving them in place for the surgeons to deal with. "He'll need some very skilled surgery to save this hand," she said aloud to Felipe, who turned his head to look, and closed his eyes convulsively at the sight of the forceps. "All that blood loss, and now a limited blood supply to the area – ah, thank God – "

Behind her the doors of the back entrance to the kitchen had swung open and men with a stretcher had come bounding in. Quickly she wrapped the wound in a triangular bandage, and then pinned it to the front of his jacket.

"Take care with this hand – uh – be very careful – " she said to the ambulance man, but he stared at her uncomprehendingly and she bit her lip, and then moving with decision, began to help the men lift the injured man.

"Felipe," she said over her shoulder, "I'd better go with this man to hospital to explain what I've done – unless there's someone else who – yes! Send at once for Pepe – Señor Delgado – "

By the time the man was safely on the stretcher Pepe

had come rushing to the kitchen and talking rapidly Isabel told him of the problem.

"They must be told at the hospital of what has happened and what I've done – can you go? Or shall I?"

"I go, of course! At once!" Pepe said with great importance. "What is it I must tell them?"

"Write it down," Isabel said, and he nodded and pulled a pen from his pocket and grabbed at the menu card one of the waiters rushed to give him when he snapped his fingers. Isabel dictated a few brief notes, warning the surgeon that the artery forceps were in position so that he did no more damage when he removed the dressing, and assuring them the man had had no drugs or stimulants at her hands. And then Pepe Delgado hurried away with the ambulance men leaving the kitchen and its staff to restore some sort of order to their afternoon.

Isabel was about to turn and leave, but as she did so she caught sight of Felipe still standing beside the wooden table. And moved fast to reach him just in time, for his face was a sick yellowish-white and he was swaying on his feet; she caught him as his eyes turned up and he fell.

"Hey – Carlos!" she called. "Now Felipe is not well! Help me!"

Together they raised Felipe and made him sit down with his head between his knees, but even though he came round very rapidly, for it was just a faint, he still looked very white.

"Poor old Felipe!" Isabel said cheerfully. "You were wonderful with that man and I'm not one whit surprised you're feeling a bit shaky now! Reaction, that's what it is. Come away to my clinic now. I'll give you a little restorative of some sort and you'll feel much better – Carlos, help me, will you?"

Obediently Felipe went with them, with Carlos leading the way down the back stairs so that none of the guests

68

should be offended by the sight of a pale and shaking maitre d'hôtel being led through their lounges, and as soon as Isabel had unlocked the clinic door Carlos led Felipe in, and helped her settle him on the couch in her office.

She gave him a mildly tranquillizing drug to swallow and then wrapped him in a blanket and told him firmly he was to sleep for a while, and that he would wake feeling quite well again and Felipe mumbled his thanks and gratefully closed his eyes, for he had indeed had a most unpleasant half hour, and was feeling more than a little queasy.

While she waited for him to fall asleep Isabel tidied her emergency bag and replaced the missing instruments, privately complimenting herself for having the foresight to put them there in the first place. Artery forceps weren't the normal equipment for such bags, but she always liked to have them available, as did most theatre trained nurses; and there was something so comforting about their sturdiness, and they had so many varied uses.

By the time she had finished and Felipe was genuinely sleeping off his shock and the drug she had given him, it was gone five thirty, and she had time to take stock of herself. Her uniform she saw with horror, was quite appallingly blood stained and besmeared; she had had no idea she had been quite so spattered. Something would have to be done about that, fast.

She peered in to the office to see Felipe snoring slightly, and looking rather better, and then moving quickly and quietly went out of the surgical room, intending to go up to her bedroom to change.

There were three people sitting in the waiting room, two women in the uniform of chambermaids, and a young man in the neat dark suit of a clerk.

"Help! I forgot to check whether anyone was here – look, I – er – entiende usted inglés?"

"I speak a little English, señorita," the clerkly boy said eagerly.

"Oh, that's grand! Now, will you explain to these ladies that I must change my uniform – there's been an accident, but all is now all right, but I must change. I will come back in ten minutes and see to all three of you. All right? Oh, yes – and ask if one of these ladies will lend me her apron – to look better as I walk through the hotel, you understand?"

He translated rapidly, and at once one of the chambermaids undid her voluminous apron and wrapped it round Isabel, nodding and smiling her willingness to lend it, and Isabel thanked her and hurried away to her room, fortunately seeing very few of the guests on the way, for most of them were out in the town shopping or lounging on the sunlit balconies and terraces at this time of the afternoon.

She changed quickly, scrubbing her shoes clean too, for they also had been marked, and feeling much more presentable hurried out of her room a bare ten minutes after going into it.

The lift wasn't there, and though she pressed the bell several times it seemed to be delayed somewhere on another floor, and too impatient to wait for it, for she was very aware of the three patients waiting for her and of Felipe sleeping peacefully in her office, she hurried to the stairs and began the long run down.

It was just as she was starting down the flight from the fourth to the third that it happened.

"Hey – you – come back here! I told you four thirty, not damned near six o'clock! And why are you going down there to look for me? Were you too damned stupid even to make sure you knew the right room number?"

Isabel looked back and up, and there, framed in a doorway that opened at the top of the staircase, was Vanda

70

Connaught, her hands on her hips, and her eyebrows raised as she looked at her.

"Ye Gods, I'd forgotten you!" Isabel said involuntarily. Indeed she had. From the moment of that phone call from the kitchen she had given Vanda Connaught not another moment's consideration.

"You did what? Are you deliberately trying to be offensive or is this your usual manner? Because either way you won't last here another five minutes! I'll see to that. Don't you dare to be so insolent, young woman! Now, come here and do as you're told, and I'll forget about your rudeness, and about your inability to keep to a time arrangement, and I won't complain to Señor Garcia," and she turned to go into her room.

"Mrs. Connaught!" Isabel stood there on the third step down, and her voice cracked like a whip. It was the same voice that had controlled many a rebellious student nurse in its time, and more than a few impudent young housemen. "I am not coming to see you. I don't give a tuppenny damn *what* you say to Señor Garcia or anyone else, and as far as I'm concerned, Madam, you are an ill-mannered, spoiled, thoroughly nasty object who is not worth my wasting my time on. I'm away now to see after the health of some people who are worth ten like you tied in a bundle – two chambermaids and a clerk and a very splendid head waiter. And if you don't like *that*, Mrs. Connaught, then you know what you can damned well do about it!"

And she turned herself and went skimming away down the stairs, leaving Mrs. Connaught in the doorway of her room with her mouth open.

Even as she dealt with her three patients, still waiting peacefully and cheerfully in the clinic, her hands were shaking with reaction, and she was glad they needed little attention that demanded a steady grip and clear mind. She

71

was seething with anger, and not a little trepidation, for however abominable the woman was, she was still a guest at the hotel. Even if Señor Garcia hadn't been the difficult man he clearly was the chances of her being bundled off home in disgrace were undoubtedly very high. And she didn't want to go, of that she was certain.

She woke Felipe at six, and sent him off back to his restaurant feeling much better and showering his gratitude and appreciation on to her. No more patients arrived to be attended to, and she tidied away the last oddments, still thinking about Vanda Connaught and the possible results of what she had said to her.

Consuelo telephoned just before six thirty.

"Isabel? I have a message for you – Señor Garcia has been all day at Valldemosa, and has telephoned me to tell you he will not require a dressing to his wound today, so you need not wait for him."

"I'd no intention of waiting for him!" Isabel said sharply. "I told him he needed daily dressings, but if he's not concerned for his own welfare, then I don't see why – "

"He had a new dressing done in Valldemosa – the doctor there," Consuelo said.

"Oh, well, it's up to him, I suppose! Anyway, thanks for letting me know, Consuelo. It was sweet of you – "

"Oh, he told me to be sure to tell you!" Consuelo said a little wickedly, and then her voice changed as she said a little haltingly, "ah – Isabel – there is a little – I think I should tell you that – "

"That Señora Connaught is waiting until Señor Garcia comes back, in order to tell him at great length about my sinfulness and demand my immediate drumming out of the hotel with my buttons pulled off, is that it?"

"Buttons? I do not understand – " Consuelo said anxiously.

72

"Och, never mind. Just a silly English saying – but am I right? About the Connaught?"

"Ah – well, yes, Isabel. It is so. I am very sorry, but I am worried for you. She is a lady who gets often her own way, and she is much the friend of Señor Garcia, you know? and I – "

"Ha! I'm no' all that surprised that they're friends!" Isabel snapped. "Just right for each other – "

"Ah, you are naughty, Isabel! I do not explain well, so you do not understand but I try – Señora Connaught and Señor Garcia they are – "

"I'm no' interested, Consuelo, I promise you! Look, if he tells me to go because of her, then he does. But I had a good reason for not going to the blasted woman's room, and if he gives me a chance to explain, then – ah, look, there's no sense in talking about it any more! Now, don't you worry, and thank you for telling me. You're a very nice kind girl."

"I hope it is all well, Isabel," Consuelo said mournfully. "I like you and I am sad if you go away. But maybe it is not so bad, hey? We wait and see – "

She was in a reckless mood as she dressed for her date with Biff, and put on the rather outrageous trouser suit in a vivid Pucci print that had so shocked the Matron of the Royal when she had worn it for the annual Christmas Dance. It was admittedly rather revealing, "but very flattering with it", she thought, as she twisted and turned in front of the mirror. "I really look rather nice."

Biff clearly agreed. He was standing in the foyer waiting for her as she came out of the lift, and smiled a long slow approving smile as she came towards him.

"You look the greatest!" he said. " I knew you were a real pretty girl, but boy – you're more than that – you're a stunner!"

"And you're very splendid, too," she said gaily, and tucked one hand into the crook of his elbow to walk off towards the door and the evening air, aware of the following stares of the guests who were strolling through the foyer, and feeling that she looked as nice as any one of them, tonight.

"I thought I'd show you the town in some style," Biff said. "If you've never seen Palma before, you ought to see it for the first time in a special sort of way – so I thought, a droshky."

"A *droshky*? But they're Russian, aren't they?"

"I know." He laughed and stepping towards the edge of the pavement waved his hat towards the far side of the square opposite. "I don't know what these are called in Spanish, but droshky sort of suits them, so that's what I call 'em!"

A brightly painted carriage with very high wheels, pulled by a brown horse wearing a colourfully vivid harness across his broad back, came towards them, making a delightful noise as harness jingled, and the bells on the horse's leathers tinkled prettily. It was one of the most storybook equipages she had ever seen in actual use, and she said so delightedly.

"Aren't they the greatest?" Biff said. "I knew you'd like it – " and he helped her to climb up into the carriage, and then joined her and wrapped the rug about her knees before leaning over to instruct the driver.

"We're going to the Pueblo Espagnol" he told her, as the horse moved forward and, swaying gently the carriage creaked into movement. "It's a sort of model village, you know? There're copies of all the different sorts of Spanish architecture, all specially built for display – really something. There's a place there, though, that's the real reason we're going. A sort of cellar – you can eat and drink, and at midnight there's a great Flamenco show

– singers and guitars and dancers – the real gypsy stuff. You'll like it, I know you will – "

For years afterwards, whenever she remembered that evening there was a special dreamlike quality about it for Isabel. The narrow winding little streets, the wide plazas, the trees and the crowds and the pavement cafés and the kiosks selling extraordinary foods and the shops and the boulevards – all drifting past the high jingling carriage and between the horse's ears jogging away far in front while Biff talked amusingly and she laughed, and drank it all in in its exciting strangeness.

And the Pueblo Espagnol, through which they strolled in the twilight, with its shuttered buildings and silent courtyards and galleried houses; it was as though they had stepped back centuries in time, and were moving about in the Spain of Don Quixote and Sancho Panza, where only windmills could make trouble for anyone, and the world was a quieter, yet more exciting romantic place.

The Flamenco cellar strengthened the feeling she had of remoteness, of not being really herself, for it was coolly whitewashed and black-beamed, looking for all the world as though it had been there for ever, and always would be.

They drank sangria, a concoction of lemonade and red wine and brandy that made her feel very gay indeed, and made the pinchitos a rabes they ate – pieces of seasoned meat cooked on skewers thrust into the vast open fire that burned in the far corner – taste incredibly exciting.

And then the dancing and the singing – she sat enchanted. The singing with its curious wailing lilt, the plink of the guitar in rhythm with the hand clapping that somehow she couldn't quite keep time with, though she tried; and above all the great stamping, clicking, whirling, dipping excitement of the dance as the girls in their black stockinged red frilled splendour moved round the tight trousered boys with their backs arched into agonizingly lovely curves, and always their faces so serious, so intent, so haughtily uncaring of the audience, for the dance was all that mattered, the dance for its own sake.

When they went back to the hotel, again riding in the high-jingling carriage, it was well after one o'clock, but she was not in the least tired. She sat there beside Biff in a dreamy contentment, staring out across the Bay at the lights of distant hotels, and the repeated gleam of the far lighthouse pulsing its warning and didn't care about anything at all. Not about the supercilious Señor Garcia, or the loathsome Vanda Connaught or – and experimentally she tried the thought, rolling it round her mind as she had rolled the sangria on her palate – or Jason Chandos.

But she shouldn't have tried that thought, for it burst the bubble of pleasure in which she had been so blissfully enclosed all night. It would all have been more than twice, more than four times as wonderful and exciting if only Jason had been with her instead of nice, friendly but oh-so-very-much-not-Jason Biff –

She turned her head to look at him as the carriage drew up outside the Hotel Cadiz, and he was smiling at her in the dim light, his wide smile that was so very friendly and comforting, and without stopping to think, she leaned forwards and very lightly kissed his cheek.

"Nice Biff. Nice, kind Biff. I *have* had a wonderful evening – so wonderful. Thank you. And goodnight – "

And before he could move she had slipped down from the high seat and run into the hotel, leaving him sitting happily grinning into the darkness.

7

The hotel foyer was still busy with people, and she could see Jaime Mendoza at the desk, talking busily to a group of very American looking guests, and she was grateful for that; there was still some magic in the evening, still a lingering sense of enchantment that she didn't want to spoil and being talked to by Jaime Mendoza would certainly do that. But as she moved towards the lift the Americans went away from the desk, and out of the corner of her eye she saw Jaime spot her, and make a move towards her. And almost without thinking she pretended she hadn't seen him and veered away towards the staircase.

She ran down rather than up, somehow not feeling at all ready for sleep, late though it was. She would go down to the swimming pool level, and sit out on the star dark terrace for a while, smelling the smells of mimosa and almond blossom and fruited trees and hugging her evening to herself a little longer.

She reached the pool level and had begun to cross the wide hallway towards the double doors that led out to the terrace when she realized that the music that had been in the background ever since she had come into the hotel was here much louder, and she turned her head and looked into the long room where the bar was, the room Consuelo had shown her that afternoon. It looked very different now, and she moved towards the doorway to stand and stare with pleasure at the transformation.

The lighting was what did it, she decided. There were lamps arranged in corners and on low tables that flanked the bar and each produced a pool of soft yellow light which gave the people round the tables a glow that was almost a halo; one blonde girl in particular caught her eye, for her hair gleamed an incredibly rich gold as the light played across it. And then she recognized her as the small Daniel-Fred's mother, and looked around further wondering briefly if the child were here too. He wasn't, but she stopped thinking about him when she saw who was.

In front of the small band of musicians that was playing on the neat dais in the corner was just one dancing couple; Sebastian Garcia, moving smoothly and elegantly in time to the soft beating of the Beguine that was being played, and clinging to him, both arms about his neck and her feet dragging a little behind his precision, Vanda Connaught. She was so close to him that it was almost as though she were trying to merge her body with his, and her head was thrown up in such a way that her lips nearly met his. And he danced precisely and smoothly on, staring down at her with his face set in the same uncompromising expressionless mould that she was beginning to realize was characteristic of him.

Watching them she tried to analyse the rush of feeling that had filled her at the sight of them. Was it revulsion at seeing a woman as drunk as Vanda Connaught so obviously was, with her not-quite-focused eyes and flushed and gleaming face? Was it seeing a middle-aged woman who should have known better behaving on a dance floor like some daft little trollop of seventeen? Or was it fear for her job, fear that this woman to whom she had been so very rude had already told Señor Garcia about it? She didn't know what the feeling was, but it was far from pleasant, and certainly had thrust out any remnants of the peace and pleasure that had been left of her evening.

"So Isabella, you like to watch the dancing, yes?" she turned her head, and saw Jaime Mendoza beaming happily at her.

"I saw you come in, and I thought – ah, now I must make my effort to make you even more at home with us, and ask you to drink with me, yes? But first, we dance – better to dance than to watch, hmm? Watching is for the old and the lazy, and not for you or me – "

And he seized her hand and pulled her into the bar and on to the dance floor almost before she realized what he was doing, and then his arms were around her and his feet moving with such energy that she had to join in if she wasn't to be tripped up to fall flat on her face.

She had to concentrate hard on his dancing, for it owed more to goodwill and hope than to any natural feeling for the beat of the music, and for a while she could not pay any attention to anything else. But then she became aware of being watched herself, and turned her head slightly to look over Jaime's shoulder.

Sebastian Garcia and Vanda Connaught had stopped dancing. She was standing clinging to his neck and staring venomously at Isabel, and even as Isabel looked at them he raised his hands to untwine her arms, and tried to move her away towards one of the tables. The music swirled louder and faster for a moment, and Jaime busily sidestepped and swooped with one carefully bent knee so that she was turned with her back to them; and then she heard it above the sound of the music, the high shrill tone she was getting to know all too well.

"So why don' you do something about it right now, Sebastian? Righ' now, you hear me? I tol' you what happened, – why don' you *do* something? That lousy

79

bitch there – it was her, don' you understand? An' you got to do somethin' about it *right away* – "

Jaime moved sideways again, and twirled her so that once again she was able to see them. He was standing very close to her at the edge of the floor, holding her arms just above the elbow, and his face was very white and still. His lips moved then, but he spoke so softly that Isabel couldn't hear his voice above the beat of the music. But she saw Vanda Connaught shake her head with the exaggerated vigour of the drunk, and her yellow hair come tumbling across her face making her look more dishevelled and unattractive than ever. And for a moment, Isabel felt very sorry for the man standing there beside her, for every line of his body showed his distaste for the situation, and his shoulders were rigid with anger.

The music stopped, and Jaime, to her intense relief, let her go and stepped back, beaming at her with every evidence of enjoyment, clearly having paid no attention at all to the little scene being played out on the edge of the dance floor.

"So, now, we have that little drink, yes?"

"No, Jaime – not tonight, if you'll forgive me," she said quickly and moved away, heading for the door. "Some other time, maybe – "

And then it happened. The sound of Vanda Connaught's voice rose again more shrill than ever and horribly clear in the big room now filled only with the sound of glasses tinkling and voices talking softly.

"If you won't do anything about it then I bloody well will – you let go of me, you hear? Tha' lousy bitch – she ought to be – "

Isabel felt her coming rather than saw her, and whirled, her hands outstretched, as Vanda Connaught came lurching across the floor towards her, her arms thrust out and the fingers positively clawed with rage.

80

"I'll scratch her bloody eyes out – " she was screeching, and people were standing up, and one of the men from the bandstand was rushing across the floor, and Isabel stood rigid with terror, for if there was one thing that always made her feel totally helpless it was physical violence –

It was Sebastian Garcia who reached her first, his hand coming over her shoulder with a dart like a snake's, and clamping down with a sharpness that made Isabel almost wince as though she'd felt it.

He pulled the woman round to face him, and with one small but very swift movement raised his hand, and the sound as his open palm struck her cheek was very clear and crisp.

There was a moment of horrified silence as Vanda Connaught stood and stared at him, her hand jerking clumsily towards her red patched face but not being able to make contact; and then her eyes rolled up rather horribly and she crumpled awkwardly to fall at his feet.

Garcia nodded crisply at the band leader who hurried back to the dais, and began to play a sprightly samba, and people talking eagerly sat down again but still kept their necks craned to see what was going on, as Garcia knelt down to pick up the sprawled figure at his feet.

"Mendoza, see to it at once that the bar serves drinks to all the guests here who have been unfortunately disturbed by this incident. My compliments, Señorita Cameron, you will be good enough to help this *ill* lady to her room. She is clearly in need of medical attention and after you have examined her, we will send for the doctor if you regard this as a necessary step."

His voice was not loud, but so clear that it could be heard everywhere in the room, even above the sound of the music, and Isabel felt the wave of relaxation that passed through the roomful of people, saw some of them look away, almost as though they were embarrassed.

"An incredible personality this," she thought briefly, obediently bending towards the recumbent Vanda Connaught. "To make people believe she's ill and not just fighting drunk, simply by saying so – "

Together they picked her up, looping an arm round each neck so that they could carry her towards the lift, and she co-operated a little, slithering her feet against the floor, and rolling her head about and mumbling a little.

They went up in the lift in total silence, standing side by side with the weight of Vanda Connaught between them, watching the floor numbers slide by, and then, as they reached her floor, carried the woman out and into her room, accompanied by the startled chambermaid who had popped her head out of her cubicle at the end of the corridor in answer to Garcia's peremptory "Criada! Venga pronto!"

He helped her put the woman on her bed and then straightened his back to stand staring down at her, his face again inscrutable.

After a moment he spoke in rapid Spanish to the chambermaid, hovering nervously at the door she had unlocked for them, and she bobbed her head and came to stand on the far side of the bed, looking expectantly at Isabel.

"The maid will help you," he said, looking at Isabel directly for the first time. "If when she is undressed and in bed you consider she needs further medical aid, be so good as to call the desk. They will arrange for a medico. For the rest – "

"Look, Señor," Isabel said awkwardly, and then bit her lip, as he stood and looked at her with his eyebrows very slightly raised. "Look, I feel a – you could say that all this – " she indicated Vanda Connaught, now snoring very unappetizingly. "I suppose it's a bit my fault – "

He raised his eyebrows a little farther. "You take a

82

great deal upon yourself, Señorita Cameron! You did not, I believe, give her the brandy she has taken tonight?"

"Well, of course, I didn't!" she said irritably. "But damn it all – I mean – I know she told you of what happened this afternoon."

"As to that, tomorrow is soon enough to discuss it. That and some other matters pertaining to your work here at the Cadiz. Now, if you will forgive me, it is late, and you as well as I have work to do before we can go to bed. Buenos noches, Señorita. If you will attend at my office tomorrow at one fifteen, these other matters will be discussed."

And he went, closing the door firmly but quietly behind him, leaving her with the help of the chambermaid and Mrs. Connaught. And by the time they had managed to undress her, as she thrashed heavily about and muttered ferociously (and Isabel was glad the maid spoke no English, feeling that it would have complicated matters considerably had so young and clearly innocent a country girl understood the obscenities that came pouring out of Vanda Connaught's lax mouth) and coped with her as she started to be violently and very unpleasantly sick, she was too tired to care what Garcia would have to say to her the next day.

And once she had assured herself that Mrs. Connaught was suffering from no more than an alcoholic stupor, was in no danger of further illness, and so did not need a doctor's care, she fell into bed feeling as desperately tired as she could ever remember being.

And woke to a sense of foreboding. She lay there in bed for a few moments after the shrilling of the telephone bell which was her morning call had stopped, staring stupidly at the bright shape of the window behind the drawn curtains, trying to remember where she was and what she was doing there.

83

And then it all came back with a rush, and she got up heavily to shower without any of the pleasure she usually took in starting the day, and to put on a crisp clean uniform. If she was going to be fired at that one fifteen interview, at least she'd go out in a blaze of glory. At which thought she grimaced at her reflection in the mirror and went down to breakfast.

But she didn't enjoy her ensaimadas and mermelada nearly as much as she had done the day before, clearly to Carlos' concern, for he hovered over her worriedly, offering her more coffee, or different ensaimadas if these were not to her taste. So that she had to pull herself out of her abstraction to reassure him she was not in any way displeased with his care of her, at which he beamed his wide smile again.

"Señorita – per favor – you tell me of the – of Ricardo? He is well this morning, si? You have discover?"

"Ricardo?"

"The butcher – se ha cortada en la mano – he cut his hand and you send to el hospital – you remember?"

She smiled at that. "I'd be hardly likely to forget! No, I don't know yet. I'll telephone the hospital in a while, and as soon as I know I'll tell all of you, yes? Uh – what's his name? Apart from Ricardo, I mean?"

"Calcagno, Señorita. Ricardo Calcagno. I tell Felipe that you telephone the message of his health, yes?"

And she agreed yes, she would, and hurried away to start her morning in the clinic, first telephoning the hospital to find out about Ricardo. But after a frustrating quarter hour she gave up, for hardly anyone seemed able to understand her halting Spanish, and those that could seemed unwilling to give her any information at all. So, in desperation she called Jaime Mendoza on her office phone, and asked him to inquire for her.

"With the greatest of pleasure, Señorita," he said

84

busily. "But tell me, the Señora Connaught – is she well again this morning? Last night – tsssss – " and he produced a hiss of enjoyable disapproval, so full of comment that she could almost see him standing there at the desk, shaking his head dolorously from side to side.

"I haven't seen her this morning. I've no doubt she's a very bad headache, though if she has it's no more than she deserves. I'll be up to see to her as soon as I've my clinic ready, and I'll report to you as soon as I have. I'll look forward to hearing the report on Ricardo, in the meantime, please."

By eight fifteen the clinic was quite ready for any patients who might present themselves, and she stood at the door for a moment, looking round with a pleasure that was sharply tempered by regret. It was such a very delightful place to work, she thought mournfully. The gentle hiss of the steam as the sterilizer bubbled contentedly to itself, the gleam of early morning sunshine on perfect chrome and glass, the faint and agreeable scent of the disinfectant that had been used to swab the terrazzo floor to a shining cleanness – already she felt proprietal about it all. It would hurt a good deal to be sent away, and not only in her pride; this job had already shown it had much satisfaction to offer in a purely professional sense –

She sighed sharply, and pulling her thoughts into a tight bundle to be tucked firmly away at the back of her mind, went quickly up to the fourth floor to Vanda Connaught's room, her emergency bag in one hand.

The room was dark when she went in, and quite abominably stuffy, and wrinkling her nose Isabel went over to open the windows, but after taking one look at the face on the pillow, left the curtains closed.

Vanda Connaught clearly was suffering quite dreadfully. Her skin had a pale greenish tint to it, and without her makeup and her usual scornful expression her face seemed as though it belonged to a wax doll that had been left out in the sun, for the flesh seemed to be melting and falling off the bones, whorled into pouches and saggy lines and creases.

Isabel moved to the bed as softly as she could and checked the pulse at the lax wrist lying on the coverlet. Firm and even, still it was a shade rapid, she thought, and after a moment's consideration, she picked up the telephone to call room service.

As she spoke quietly giving an order for a drink to be brought to the room, Vanda Connaught woke and moved her head on the pillow to groan a little, and then lie still, her face crumpled with pain.

"My head – " she murmured as Isabel leaned over her. "My God, my *head* – "

"Ay, I've no doubt it's pretty nasty," Isabel said dryly, and Mrs. Connaught opened her eyes and squinted up at her, only to shut them again in pain.

"You – is it? Get the hell out of here, you. I don't want to see you anywhere near me – " and then she rolled over, and Isabel, recognizing the signs, rushed to the bathroom and was back with a bowl just in time.

By the time Mrs. Connaught was leaning back on her pillows whiter than ever – if that were possible – and exhausted, the waiter had arrived with a glass on a tray, and Isabel took it from him, and slipping one arm behind her shoulders so that she had to sit up, made the other woman drink it. She grimaced horribly, and tried to pull her head away, but Isabel was determined, and despite her spluttering made her drink it all, as the waiter stood grinning hugely and watching with undisguised pleasure, until Isabel saw him and with a sharp "Basta! Marchesé!" sent him away.

"God Almighty, what *was* that? It tasted like boiled garbage or something – " Mrs. Connaught gasped, but already her face was a little less wan and her voice stronger.

"Fernet Branca," Isabel said, and went to the bathroom to bring a bowl of fresh water and towels, to set about washing the sick woman. "Tastes poisonous, but works very well indeed. You're feeling better already." It was a statement, not a question.

There was a pause as the other woman let Isabel swab and dry her face before starting on her hands and arms and chest.

"You're right. I do." She moved her head experimentally on her pillow, but winced again.

"I'd not try to cavort about too much, all the same," Isabel said. "It'll take you a few hours yet to get this little matter out of your system. Go on like this, and you'll be suffering from chronic alcohol poisoning, you know that?"

"Ay, I know it fu' well!" Mrs. Connaught said, sneeringly imitating Isabel's Scots accent. "And it's no bloody business of yours."

"If I've to hold your head when you're sick, I think it could be said to be partly my business," Isabel said equably, as she cleared away the washing things, and then began to make the bed with swift professional movements. "Not that I'll be here that long to do it, of course, will I? I daresay you're very pleased with yourself about *that*, aren't you?"

Mrs. Connaught opened her eyes wide and stared up at the face above her for a moment, and then made an odd grimace, half pout, half "couldn't-care-less" shrug. "That's what *you* think, you silly – oh, for God's sake get the hell out of here, will you? I've had enough of you to last me a life time. Get out – "

"If you need me at all during the day, the switchboard will put you through to the clinic," Isabel said, quietly.

"I'll be up to see you again at midday, and in the meantime I'll arrange for some tea and dry toast to be sent up. If you've any sense you'll take it. You'll feel a lot better when you have. Good morning to you, Mrs. Connaught."

All through the clinic hours she wondered and worried about Vanda Connaught's odd reaction. "That's what *you* think – " What did she mean by that? Surely she had made sure that her friend Garcia *was* going to sack her? But then, she remembered the way Sebastian Garcia had looked last night, staring down at Vanda Connaught lying sprawled on the floor, and she wondered even more –

And then she had to concentrate on work as the clerk from the afternoon before came in to be her next patient; and as she set about redressing the small boil on the back of his neck, he set about practising his small grasp of English on her.

"All the people in the hotel, they talk of the Señorita, the new enfermera – the nurse, in English, yes? All the people – the staff you understand – talk and talk – "

"Well, new people on the staff anywhere always make people talk," Isabel said easily. "How does that poultice feel? Not too hot? Good – we should be able to open this in the morning, and then you'll have a great deal less trouble with it. Well, I hope they'll get over the newness of having a nurse on the premises soon. When too many people talk about my being here there'll be too many curious people wasting time coming down with very small complaints that don't need a nurse!"

"Oh, but for me, it is very necessary!" the boy said anxiously. "Indeed it is – what is it – very, very bad. It makes much pain, yes? It is for me very – "

"Och, I know!" Isabel said, and laughed as she fastened the dressing securely. "I didn't mean you! Now, away with you, and come tomorrow at twelve – no earlier. Then I'll lance that boil, and you'll be fine – "

88

As long as I'm here to do it for you, that is, she thought sourly, as she cleared up after him, and dealt with the few instruments that needed sterilizing. The way things are at the moment, though, I just don't know (what the hell *did* she mean? "That's what *you* think – ") and then irritated with herself, she set about treating the last two or three patients before doing a final clean up, and washing her hands and combing her hair ready for the forthcoming interview with Sebastian Garcia.

She looked as neat and as efficient as she possibly could when she was ready to leave the clinic, with only the faintest hint of lipstick to soften the severity of her unmade up face, and her hair pulled firmly back under the pretty lacy cap.

But despite her cool crisp and highly professional appearance her heart was thumping heavily in her throat and her legs had a fine tremble in them as she made her way up the stairs to Sebastian Garcia's office at precisely a quarter past one.

8

She walked straight into his office, not waiting for an answer to the perfunctory tap she had made on the heavy glass door, holding her head high and with her face set, she knew perfectly well, in a mulish expression.

But she was so startled at what she saw when she closed the door behind her that she blinked, and let her mouth soften until she knew it was hanging open in surprise. For the room seemed full of people; there behind the large desk was Sebastian Garcia, with Consuelo standing attentive and poised for action just behind his left shoulder. On his other side stood Felipe, and beyond him the head chef, looking quite incredibly huge in his whites and his tall hat. In front of the desk three other men were sitting, all looking remarkably alike with their smooth olive-skinned faces and pleasantly rotund bellies, their sleek black hair, neat dark suits, blazing white shirts and sober dun coloured ties.

They stood up as she came in, and bobbed their heads towards her with such chorus-like precision that for a moment she wanted to giggle, but then the amusement died in her throat as she looked round at the solemn faces all staring at her.

"Did y'have to call up the whole regiment to drum me oot?" she said involuntarily, and then frowned and bit her lip, hearing the Scots burr in her voice and knowing how close she was to exploding into anger.

"Buenos dias, Señorita," Sebastian Garcia said, standing up. "Regiment? I am afraid I do not quite understand?"

"It's no matter," she said stiffly. "You wanted to see me at one fifteen, so it's one fifteen and here I am. I'd be grateful if you'd say what you have to say and be done wi' it. I must say that I didna' expect to see quite so many people."

She looked sideways at the three round dark men, all still standing and staring gravely at her and wondered briefly; Directors? Sleeping partners? and then firmed her mouth: she was damned if she cared one way or the other. Let them just get on with it –

"Permit me to introduce everybody, Señorita." He came round the desk to stand beside her. "May I present Señor Castillo, Señor Zumel, Señor Gomez. They wish to speak to you on a matter of some importance."

One of the men stepped forwards and coughed self-importantly and with a small bow towards Sebastian Garcia began to speak in careful Spanish, waiting after a few sentences for Garcia to interpret.

"Señor Castillo is the senior surgeon at the hospital to which Ricardo Calcagno was admitted yesterday."

Señor Castillo spoke again, clearly enjoying every moment of his speech, and still looking quite preternaturally solemn, and again Sebastian Garcia translated, with his usual air of total imperturbability.

" – the patient, he is happy to tell you, is comparatively well this morning – he underwent surgery after admission – the operation, performed by Señor Zumel – " (Here one of the other men produced a sharp little bow) " – lasted for three hours – the hand did not need amputation as was first feared – "

Now the Spanish was coming faster, and more excitedly, as Señor Castillo waved his arms about, and Sebastian

91

Garcia had to speak more loudly to be heard above the other's voice. " – and although Calcagno required several pints of blood in transfusion, his outlook is extremely good. The doctors of the hospital have come to express – they are very anxious to express – their appreciation of the excellent first aid care you gave – it is an undoubted fact that you saved this man's life and the hand – without such intelligent care – he would quite certainly have lost his livelihood – if not his life – and – "

At this point Garcia frowned sharply at something the little round man had said, and shook his head, but Señor Castillo became even more excited and insistent, and Garcia shrugged slightly and went on " – and should you be willing to leave the post of clinic nurse at the Hotel Cadiz, they at the hospital would be very happy, indeed honoured – to welcome you to the staff as nurse in charge of the operating theatres – "

And then they were all staring at her again, and now she couldn't help it; the laughter born of tension and embarrassment that had started building up in her throat as soon as she realized what was going on could be contained no longer, and she had to let it escape into a soft snort, and her face creased into a wide grin as she looked from one to the other and tried to control her mirth.

After a moment during which the three men stared at her in some bewilderment they too began to grin, and then Felipe and the chef started to laugh and within moments they were all – with the exception of Garcia who returned to his seat behind his desk, and Consuelo were all laughing and nodding at her.

She caught her breath at length and blew her nose, and smiled at the three doctors ("and if only they didn't look like some music hall act it wouldn't be so bad," she thought, as the laughter came bubbling up again, but this time was more easily controlled) and said aloud "Please, forgive me gentlemen. I didn't mean to laugh quite so – you caught me by complete surprise, you see. And when I'm startled I always laugh – I'm truly sorry to have seemed so – so silly." She looked a little wickedly at Sebastian Garcia and smiled again. "And apart from anything else, when I came in here this morning I thought it was to be fired – "

Calmly he translated her words to the three doctors, though quite obviously leaving out the comment about being fired, and they smiled and nodded at her, all in high good humour.

"As for coming to the hospital to work," she said, making her voice sound as friendly as she could. "Really, I am very honoured, but if you'll forgive me, I think not. I like my post here at the Cadiz very much, and I'd be very sad to leave it – " and again she couldn't resist giving a wicked glance at Sebastian Garcia.

But he ignored it, merely translating her words, and the three doctors looked momentarily disappointed, though clearly not unduly surprised and smiled at her in great friendliness.

Señor Gomez put his hand into his pocket and pulled out a small bundle and stepping forwards smartly put it into her hand, and she gazed at it for a moment in horror; surely they weren't going to give her some sort of gift? That would be too much.

"Please, gentlemen, all this fuss!" she said. "I did nothing all that special – just the job I'm here to do. And that I was trained for – " Tentatively she unwrapped the bundle and then laughed aloud in relief, for it contained the two pairs of artery forceps she had used for Calcagno's wound, and she held them up to show everyone.

"They're very honest at the hospital to return your instruments so punctiliously, Señor Garcia!" she said gaily, and he nodded, and repeated her words in Spanish, and the three doctors shrugged deprecatingly and smiled, and she smiled back.

Then Felipe and the chef suddenly stepped forwards, and with the same rather quaint formality the doctors had displayed, Felipe thanked her on behalf of the kitchen staff – interpreting, he said, for his colleague the chef, Señor Hernandez – and himself, for he much appreciated the care she had given him, and assured her that the staff felt very happy to know she was there and so capable of dealing with the type of accident that could so easily happen in a busy kitchen and restaurant and –

"Thank you, Felipe," Sebastian Garcia cut in quietly. "I believe Señorita Cameron quite understands your appreciation."

"Oh, indeed – yes, I do," Isabel said breathlessly, beginning to wish the floor would open and swallow her, so ludicrously embarrassing was the whole business becoming. "Indeed, Felipe, it was kind of you to say so much – and it was a pleasure, really – I mean – oh, you know what I mean!"

And then, at last, they were all gone, the three doctors bowing themselves out, and offering invitations, through Sebastian Garcia's clipped interpretation, to visit the hospital at any time she wanted, and then Felipe and the chef departed, followed by Consuelo who beamed happily at her from the door, and then closed it softly behind her.

"Och, that was *dreadful*!" she said, taking a deep breath, and he indicated a chair for her to sit in as he came back from the door to reseat himself at his desk. "If only I'd been warned what it was all about, it wouldna' have been so bad! But as it was – " and gratefully she sat in the chair, and held her hands to her hot cheeks.

"Dreadful? In what way? These doctors are very senior

members of the hospital staff, and that they should come on a busy day to speak to you of their approval of your work is hardly dreadful."

"Oh, I appreciate the compliment they paid me!" she said quickly. "Look, please don't think I was being – oh, rude or contemptuous, saying that! It's just that – damn it, I'm a Scot! I'm not used to such – such *fussing*. It was a job I had to do and I did it, and all this – well, for me, it was dreadful and I can't deny it! But of course I appreciate what they said. It was very kind."

He was sitting turning a paper-knife between his fingers, staring down at it, the bandage on his hand looking very white against his tanned skin, and there was a moment's silence before he spoke. When he did she was startled to hear the note of uncertainty that was in his voice; that Sebastian Garcia, the chilly, the still, the expressionless Garcia should sound uncertain was almost incredible.

"You said you would be sad to leave the Cadiz. That you were happy here. That was true?"

"True? Of course it was. I'm no' in the habit of tellin' lies!" she said, and embarrassment sharpened her voice.

"It could have been courtesy." And now he raised his heavy lids and looked very directly at her, and she thought with sudden inconsequence "his eyes really are incredibly dark. And very attractive – " and blinked and looked away, startled by the sudden wave of shyness that swept through her.

"I told you, I'm a Scot," she said after a moment. "We don't go in for such niceties. Dour, that's what we are. So even if it were a terrible insult to tell the truth, I'd be likely to tell the truth all the same."

"I am very glad to hear that," he said gravely. "It makes my situation a great deal more easy."

She looked briefly at him, and again her eyes had to

slide away. "Oh!" she said. And couldn't think of anything more to say.

There was another long pause and then he said softly "You said also you expected to be – er – fired. That too, then, was true?"

She nodded silently.

"A foolish question, since already you have explained your national characteristics – so I ask you another one. *Why* did you expect so remarkable an action?"

"*Why?*" she stared at him in amazement. "Why? Oh, come on, Señor Garcia! I'm no' daft, you know! After what happened with that – with Mrs. Connaught? I was sure that you'd – I mean, not only is she a guest here, but she's a special friend of yours, isn't she? And although I had an awfu' lot of provocation, I was damned rude to her! So of course I expected – I mean, who wouldn't?"

"Who told you Señora Connaught was a special friend of mine?" he said sharply.

"Who? I don't know – one or two people – I really can't be sure," she shrugged. "But she is, isn't she? *I'd* certainly got that impression, anyway!"

"Because of last night?" Again he looked at her with that heavy-lidded directness that made her shiver slightly. "Would it surprise you to know that it was my intention this morning to apologize to *you* for the appalling behaviour of Señora Connaught last night, and to ask you to remain here at the Cadiz in spite of her?"

"Surprise me? – Sur – I should say it would!" she said weakly.

"Then clearly the people who have given you this absurd gossip about Señora Connaught and myself are remarkably effective liars! It is as well that you cannot recall who told you this – though I suspect I can guess – since I would be most angry with that individual were I to know! Although – "

He stood up and moved across the room to stand beside his office window, staring out at the street. "Perhaps it is in part my own fault. They know only what they see. I do not ever tell people of my personal affairs, or of those matters that do not concern them. You, however – " he turned to look at her again. "I wish to tell *you*. And after you have heard, I trust you will be able to accept the apology I offer on behalf of Mrs. Connaught, and also accept with calmness any – future – unpleasantness she creates. So – "

He came back to his desk and sat down, leaning forwards to speak very directly to her, and she sat feeling for all the world like a mesmerized rabbit, watching his face as he talked. But rather liking what she saw.

"Vanda Connaught is the widow of a man who was, many years ago, my partner. Unfortunately he was a bad partner – a poor businessman, and an alcoholic. This I did not realize at the time, being a young man of little experience. I believed if I worked hard, and was thrifty and frugal – the good peasant qualities, yes? – all would prosper. But, to my surprise I did not prosper, and it was some time before I discovered that the so charming Bill Connaught is an alcoholic who uses the company money and makes trouble for me. So, I start – quietly, since I wish no problems – to raise the money to buy out of his partnership the useless Bill Connaught. You must not misunderstand me – the man was my friend, and I liked him. But as a business partner – tssss – " and he produced that characteristic Spanish sound. "So, I raised the money, and I arranged with Bill to buy him out. But he tells me I may not tell Vanda until all is completed for she will be very angry with him. She was not then as heavy a drinker as her husband, all those years ago, and she had still hopes of reforming him – " He looked remote for a moment, and then went on stiffly, "Although in my

97

impatience and youth I am convinced that this is not ever to be. So – "

He stopped, and dropped his eyes to his clasped hands again and then after a second looked up at her, and his face was more relaxed now, an almost rueful expression on it.

"So, Bill takes the money, and I own entirely the Cadiz operation. This is long before we have so splendid an edifice as the present Cadiz, you understand – then we are little more than a pensión. In seven years, much can happen – So, as I say, Bill takes the money and because Vanda does not know, he goes on a – I do not know the English word – he drinks like – like a crazy man – "

"He went on a bender? A binge?" Isabel said.

"Is that what it is called? I will remember. So, he went on a bender. And was drowned because on one mad night he takes a boat from the Bay and goes out to the sea in it like a – like a twice crazy man." He shrugged, "It was I suppose, inevitable, one day, that such a thing should happen. For Bill I think it was as he wanted. He died feeling himself to be great and important and filled with the glory that is the wine – "

There was a long silence, and then she said softly, "And Vanda? His wife?"

He looked at her and shrugged. "What could I do? She did not know that Bill had sold out to me. In her grief, how could I tell her? And knowing that his death was partly my fault – no – do not argue." For she had opened her mouth to speak. "It was in part. If I had not given him the money, no – bender, no boat, no drowning."

"And you've never told her," she said.

"No. I have never told her. She lives here, but tells everybody she is here for just the season – but the years go by and still she is here. I buy for her gifts – jewellery, clothes, you understand – as her share of the profits of the partnership, I tell her. She has, as you have seen, herself become a woman tied to the brandy bottle. She has become very stupid – "

"Not all that stupid," Isabel said, suddenly realizing what Vanda Connaught had meant by her "That's what *you* think – " She had known somehow, that Sebastian Garcia was not going to dismiss her.

"Oh, but yes. The drink has spoiled the brains she has. But I must thank God she never asks for the books or to see the business arrangements. If she did, and she found out that she is in fact penniless, that she received from me a form of charity – she was once a woman of pride and charm as well as brain, when I knew her first. I have much to answer for, I feel, for the state she is in."

"Then you're daft," Isabel said vigorously. "Really daft. I can see why you should feel responsible for her, but all the same your own good sense surely tells you it wasn't really your fault that her husband died! You said as much yourself!"

"I know. Indeed, I do know. But the brain and the feelings do not always work together, you understand."

"No, they don't," she said after a moment, and pushed down a sudden vivid memory of Jason saying, "But you've got to be sensible, Isabel!" and her own passionate rejection of any such unfeeling consideration –

"So, there you have the account of the problem of Señora Connaught. I must tell you that in the past years I have lost many good staff because she is so impossible a lady. But I have shrugged and said lo qué será. What must be, you understand? Even the best of staff can be replaced. Usually."

He looked up and for the second time since she had met him, he smiled, and as it transformed his face, lifting it out of its normal stern lines, she felt herself melt towards him. It was quite absurd, and she knew it, but all the animosity she had allowed to build up during these few brief days since she had come to the Cadiz disappeared under the influence of that smile.

"Usually. But you – I did not want to risk losing you. I do not think you will be so easy to replace. Not only because of the way you dealt with the kitchen accident yesterday, or because of the way all the staff are talking of you with such liking, such trust – " she felt the red tide begin to mount in her cheeks. "But for – there are reasons. So, you will accept my apology? And will be able to tolerate the behaviour of the Señora Connaught should she again make so disgraceful a scene as last night's? It is important to me that you should say yes."

"Oh, of course I understand!" she said, and she knew her voice sounded shaky and couldn't for the life of her do anything about it. "I've dealt with more difficult types than Mrs. Connaught in my time, I promise you! And now I know something about why she's so disagreeable – oh, there'll be no problems, I promise you. And – er – I'm delighted you want me to stay at the Cadiz. I truly do like it here, and the clinic is beautiful, and the staff – it's really very nice, and the town and all – "

She was floundering and chattering on and on in her sudden nervousness and she knew it and in an effort to behave more like her usual crisp self she stood up and smoothed her uniform, ready to turn towards the door and escape.

"So I'll be away now" she said, still gabbling a little. "And I'll be in the clinic soon after I've taken my lunch, if you want to come early to have your wound dressed. I know it was done in Valldemosa yesterday, but I think I ought to see it today, all the same – "

He stood up and came round the desk to hold the door open for her, and he stood there for a moment looking down at her with that same disturbing smile on his face.

"But of course it is necessary for you to see it. You,

100

after all are the surgeon in charge of this case! I will indeed come to the clinic this afternoon. But before you go, I wish to make amends to you for another small episode that I have since realized could perhaps have been not quite understood. Tonight, Señorita, it would give me much pleasure to escort you to an evening of entertainment. I wish myself to accompany you, you understand – I do not merely offer you the use of my car and chauffeur. I do very much hope you will come with me. There is much of our beautiful island that I would wish to show you – "

She smiled up at him, her face filled with laughter. "Oh, I'd like that – I really would! And as for the car and the chauffeur and that – pfui! I made a right wee fool of mysel' that night! I'll be glad to forget it if you will!"

He held out his hand to her, and she took it and let her fingers rest in the cool firmness of his grasp for a moment.

"You are more than generous to me, for I behaved very poorly that evening. So, hasta la vista! Until we see each other again – " and he squeezed her fingers gently, almost imperceptibly, and opened the door for her.

She went through, knowing her cheeks were red and hoping there would be no one outside to stare and conjecture, and then his voice pulled her back.

"Señorita Cameron – I trust that this invitation tonight – it will not cause any – ah – difficulty with your caballero – Señor Squires was his name, I believe?"

And now her face was a very rich scarlet indeed and she said quickly, "Caballero! Heavens, no! He's not a boyfriend. Just someone I met on the plane – uh – hasta la vista, señor!" and she fled, knowing quite well he was watching her all the way across the broad foyer. And finding a very definite satisfaction in the knowledge.

101

9

She sat with her elbows on the table, her chin propped on her clasped hands, and watched fascinated, as the men came pouring out of the kitchens at the far end, each carrying high aloft a long sword flaming with scarlet and yellow fire, watched them separate and come running down the sides of the great table to stand in rows behind the diners, still holding their burdens high.

"It's beautiful," she breathed, and then laughed, as she looked at him. "But it'll surely be unfit to eat by the time the fire's out?"

"Watch," he said. "You will see," and even as he spoke, the men moved, dipped their swords and twisted them, and although she couldn't see how it happened, suddenly the flames were doused, and then each man stepped forwards to serve his own pair of diners. She moved sideways as their man leaned across her shoulder, and she felt her breath catch suddenly as her arm touched Sebastian's. "This is absurd!" she told herself sternly, "to go all flibberty and silly like some green girl just beause I've touched him – " but she enjoyed the sensation of shivery pleasure all the same.

The waiter, using a long fork with great dexterity, slid some of the meat impaled on the sword on to her plate, and then moved on to serve Sebastian. And almost as soon as he'd gone away another waiter arrived with great wooden bowls of salad and dishes of olives, black and wrinkled and gleaming on dark green lettuce leaves, and hot baked potatoes.

"Good food, yes?" he watched her as she tasted the meat, and laughed aloud at the startled look on her face when he added, "It is sucking pig – "

"Oh, no! It seems awful to eat such young animals!"

"And in your country do you not eat lamb? So – why not the young pig? It is a delicacy of this country, especially cooked in this manner over the open spit – in the old days all the farmhouses and country people had a barbecue pit always in use."

As they ate he talked more, telling her fascinating tales of the history of the Island, of the invasions of the Moors, of the long distant but still not forgotten wars of centuries ago when great princes sailed to the Island, and beautiful proud women fought beside their lords and masters to defend the land they owned –

It was all very romantic and as she ate, and drank the acrid but fragrant red wine, she felt again the curious enchantment creep over her, the same enchantment she had found in her evening with Biff, when they had watched flamenco gypsies dance and walked among the recreated haciendas and town houses of old Spain.

"It's something about the place itself," she told herself, staring up at the high stone walls of the vast farmhouse barn they were in, together with many other holiday-making diners, and at the great open fireplace in the centre where the spits turned with the small carcases of the animals roasting smokily above the leaping flames. "Watch yoursel' Isabel Cameron. Don't be pushed into deep water by a lot of romantic stuff and nonsense – "

But however much her Calvinist conscience whispered its warning in her ear, she didn't care. She was in Spain, in Spring, sitting with a delightfully handsome – and – admit it! – devastatingly attractive man who quite patently found her equally interesting. And she smiled at him, knowing as a woman always does know that her skin and hair gleamed richly and becomingly in the soft candlelight of the vast hall, and that her green eyes were reflecting the leaping flames of the barbecue.

He looked at her very closely for a long moment, over the rim of the wine glass that he was holding to his lips, and his eyes seemed darker and more hooded than ever in the dimness. Abruptly he put his glass down, and put his hand out to take hers in a firm warm grip.

"We have eaten enough," he said curtly. "Come. I show you more – "

And then they were moving away from the great table, and some of the people there waved and called and raised their wine glasses at them knowingly, and for a second she held back, pulling against his grasp, but he urged her gently forwards, and she thought recklessly "Ah, what does it matter? So I'm being a daft romantic, and why not? Why not?"

"Because you're supposed to be here to get over Jason, not to get tangled with a new man," the little voice whispered at her but the other half of her retorted " – and what better way to be cured than to be taken away into a soft Spanish night to be kissed by a handsome Spaniard? – " For she suddenly had no doubt that this was what he wanted to do, that this was why he had taken her away from the table so suddenly, and she was glad of the little wine she had taken; not enough to alter her thinking but enough to lessen her intrinsic shyness –

They were outside now, walking across the great flagged courtyard in the light of lanterns hung on the high walls of the buildings that flanked it, and he was holding her elbow now in the firm grasp that made that small secret place inside her shiver again and again.

At the far side of the courtyard, where the shadows

104

were thickest he stopped, and she felt him move closer beside her and suddenly the agreeable shiver became less agreeable, seemed to be a sick feeling, and moving abruptly she turned away from him.

But at the same moment he had moved from her side, and gone forwards, and now she could see that he had pushed open a huge wooden door, could hear it creaking as a square of smokey light was etched against the blackness.

"In there," he said in the same clipped tones. "You will see." And uneasily but obediently she stepped forwards into the light.

They were in a stable, a vastly high beamed stable with whitewashed walls against which harness hung in rich leathery strands, and brasses shone satin smooth in the lamplight, where sweet hay was piled on the beaten earth floor in casual mountains that glowed a soft greenish yellow. She could see the gentle brownness of wood beyond, beams and pillars of ancient notched wood marching in quiet rows across the huge space, to make a row of stalls inside which she could see them as well as hear them; beautiful long maned yellow-white horses, with restless heads moving against the darkness, their eyes shining white and frightened as they snickered and whinnied softly.

He moved across the straw-strewn floor to lean over one of the stalls and take the nose of one of the most nervous of the animals in his hand, and he whispered and murmured gently, and then after a moment, when she had quieted and was gently nuzzling his hand, her absurdly long lashed great eyes losing the white stare of suspicion that had first filled them, he leaned down and unlocked the door.

Isabel watched them both as he led the animal out, the sleek black slenderness of the man against the tense quivering muscles of the mare; watched them stand together for a while, the horse moving one fore-foot with elegant fretfulness against the floor, while still nuzzling the man's neck, and thought, "He's beautiful – too beautiful – " and then just stood and watched them, grateful for the beauty of the sight.

"She is a splendid lady, this lady, yes? My Donna Clara, I call her – of all the animals in this stable she is the one for whom I have most love. You understand this, yes? You told me of your childhood in those Scottish hills of yours. You are a farmer's daughter – you must know of horses too? This is why I brought you here. To see my lovely Donna Clara – "

She moved forwards to come to stand by the horse and put her hand up gently to touch her velvet nose, and after a moment of eye-rolling anxiety Donna Clara settled and let Isabel rub her nose and caress her sensitive twitching ears.

"We have horses, yes, but nothing like this," she said softly. "I rode a very solid little brown cob at home. She was a friendly animal, and as tough and rocky as our hills and I loved her, but this – Oh, she's very special."

"She is a palomino," Sebastian said gravely, and then turning her gently led her back to her stall. "She is not entirely my property, you understand. They will not sell her to me! She belongs here to the farm, and she is one of the team of animals that do dressage – the performance of skilled riding, you understand?"

"Oh, I know! Even in distant Scotland we've heard of the skills of Spanish horses and their riders!"

He smiled then, across the mare's head, as he relocked the stall. "Of course. I am sorry. But so often, you know, people who come to the Island have no knowledge of these things. This is why I explain – "

With a last caress for Donna Clara's nose he turned away, and came back to her and they walked out into

106

the darkness again, which seemed much blacker now; and he closed the door and again taking her arm in that now familiar grip led her back through the shadows to the dining hall, where now there was the music of guitars and accordians and the sound of laughter and chatter as people danced on the square of grooved stones around the barbecue fire, and the waiters scurried about with trays of drinks.

"I particularly wished you to see my Donna Clara," he said, as they stood in the doorway and she blinked at the light and smoke. "For it is important to me that you are also interested in horses."

He looked down at her, and as though he had actually pulled her round to face him, she looked up to meet his serious dark gaze. "One day soon you shall come and ride with me. There are other good mares here who will bear you well. We shall ride and you will find the difference between your little Scottish cob and our highbred Spanish palomino ladies. But now – we dance, yes?"

And with a sudden gaiety he took her hand and drew her forward and they were dancing, and whether it was the headiness of the atmosphere or the strange beating lilt of the music or the specialness of his dancing she never knew; but she danced as she never had, feeling as light as dandelion down, letting the music move into her bones and merge with them, telling her feet to go where they wanted, swooping and bending to the guiding pressure of his hand on the small of her back, dreamily yet exhilaratedly floating her way through and with and beyond the sound of music.

It was late when they stopped dancing, and drank some coffee laced with rum – "to keep out the chill of the evening" he said gravely. "It is still only February, you must remember, and the nights can be treacherous here" – and made their way back to the car.

His chauffeur, an elderly man who seemed to communicate only in grunts, was waiting for them and they drove back through the darkness, side by side and silent. But it was a companionable silence that had nothing of shyness in it. She just sat there with her head resting back against the squabs of the leather upholstery, dreamily watching the dark trees and small houses beside the road swish by, and relaxed happily.

Until she remembered the way she had been convinced Sebastian had been about to kiss her, out there in the darkness of the farmyard, and was glad now of the darkness of the car, for she felt the hot colour flood up her cheeks. And then, as so often happened, her native humour took over, and she laughed softly in her throat at her own absurdity.

"And it is permitted that I share the joke?" His voice came suddenly loud in the darkness and she turned her head to peer at him. "No joke," she said easily. "I was happy, that is all. So I laughed."

"You are interesting people, you Scottish ladies," he said, and she could hear the amusement below the surface of his voice, "You laugh when you are startled, you laugh when you are happy – when else do you laugh?"

"When I'm stupid – " she said, suddenly sharp, for it had happened again. Again an unwanted memory had come curling up from the depths of her mind. There was Jason, sitting and staring anxiously at her, and saying again "You do see what I mean, Isabel? You do understand? It's not that I don't love you – God knows I do – but I just can't go on doing this to you – " and herself, laughing in a crisp offhand sort of way, and shrugging her shoulders and saying "Oh, I suppose I know when I'm beaten, Jay! I've done all I could, pleaded all I'm about to. From here on it's just a great big joke," and she had laughed again.

"When I'm stupid," she repeated, and then gave herself

a little shake. "It was a lovely evening, Señor Garcia. Thank you for taking me," she said formally, and now it was his turn to laugh softly in the darkness.

"You sound now like a very well brought up Spanish young lady. Such careful etiquette! Please, you will now call me Sebastian, yes? It is my name. And you – I will call you Isabella – so Spanish a name, Isabella – " and there was a note in his voice as he said it that made that little shiver of pleasure come back again.

"By all means," she said lightly. "Except, if you'll forgive me, in working hours. I'd not be too happy about being anything but very proper and correct then – "

"But of course!" he said equally lightly, and then lapsed into silence for the rest of the journey into Palma.

He led her into the hotel and to the entrance to the lift, apparently quite oblivious of the swift knowing glances of the guests and staff who were still about, and shook hands with her gravely to say goodnight. And, after a moment of hesitation, raised her hand and brushed the back of it with his lips.

"Your company has been an enchantment, Señorita Isabella," he said softly. "And soon, I hope we will be able to repeat our evening. Buenas Noches, Señorita."

"Buenas Noches," she said, and turned to walk into the lift, which had now arrived and was standing, doors open waiting for her. And then as she pressed the button and the doors closed she added swiftly "Hasta la vista!" and saw the rare smile break out across his face again. And she went on, up to bed in her lovely cool room feeling a delicious contentment, and a great deal more happy than she had been that morning when she left it.

She had almost finished the morning clinic next day when the telephone on her desk rang.

"Well, hi, Isabel! How *are* you?"

"Biff! How nice of you to call. I'm fine, thanks! How are *you*? Working hard?"

"No more'n I have to!" he said gaily, but then his voice changed a little. "Oh – I called by last night to see how you were. I thought maybe we could go out again, you know? You were very sweet the other night, Isabel, and well – I just thought. But they told me you were out. With that Señor Garcia. So, I was a bit – well, you were pretty hot against that guy the last time we spoke, so I thought maybe the man at the desk had it all wrong – "

"No, he had it right, Biff," she said, and then looking over her shoulder at the waiter she had left sitting patiently with a bandage half applied said quickly: "It's a long story, Biff, and I can't stop now. I have a patient waiting – "

"Gee, I'm sorry!" he sounded so contrite that she felt guilty herself for having upset him. "Look, I'll call by tonight, okay? We'll go have a drink and a meal at one of the little bodegas I know – like, taverns? and we can talk – I'll pick you up at around eight thirty, okay?" and the phone clicked and then buzzed as he hung up.

As she finished the clinic she wondered briefly whether she should have accepted that date with Biff, and then shrugged her doubts away. It wasn't as though she owed him any sort of special loyalty, she told herself. I mean, if Sebastian asks me out again I'll go, just as I'm going out with Biff. There's nothing special about either of them, is there? Not like the days when I was with Jason; then to have made a date with someone else would have seemed to her impossible, the worst kind of disloyalty. And anyway, she'd never had eyes for anyone but Jason, then –

Sebastian came for a renewal of his dressing just before lunch, and as she took off the bandage and examined his wound she thanked him politely for the previous evening's entertainment. It was somehow easier to do so while she had her head bent over his hand.

"It was indeed a great pleasure for me, Señorita Cameron," he said gravely, and she looked up swiftly and smiled at his careful observance of her own rule about the formal use of names in working hours, and he smiled back, fully understanding her amusement.

"It occurred to me that on Sunday next if you wished it we could return to the farmhouse to ride. We are not yet too far into the season, and I will not be too busy on Sundays for at least another month or two – so I would like to use the opportunity and show you the paces of the horses, and also to show you the Island's great beauty – the almond blossom. It is nearly at its best, and it will be very agreeable to take you to the almond groves and let you see the loveliness of the blossom. We will take a picnic, yes? It will be very enjoyable."

And she agreed it would and pushed her vague sense of unease about Biff to the back of her mind. There were no rules that said she couldn't enjoy the company of both men, and enjoy it she would, she told herself firmly, as she locked the clinic and went to lunch. Enjoy it she *would*.

She had swum and sunbathed and swum again, and was lying spreadeagled on the warm mattress, letting the sun lick her skin dry and filling her nose with the mingled smells of flowers and fruit and hot dust when the orange light behind her lids darkened to a deep red, and she opened her eyes to squint upwards.

A small boy was standing with his legs apart and his fists on his diminutive hips, staring down at her.

"Hello, Fred," she said. "How are you? Enjoying your holiday?"

He scowled heavily, and then squatted down beside her to pick at the sand between the flagstones with restless fingers.

"All right, I s'pose," he muttered.

She sat up, and curling her arms round her knees looked

111

on the rough curly head, and smiled a little. "What's gone wrong with it? No other people your own age to play with? I saw quite a few sensible looking types about who looked around ten, like you."

He beamed up at her then, and she knew her intended compliment had hit its target. "Well, *akshully*, I'm not quite eight. And those other fellas they're nearly nine and you'd think they was the only people in the *world* the way they go on." He brooded darkly for a moment. "I mean, why shouldn't a person who's nearly eight be as good as a person who's nearly nine? Why shouldn' he? An' when I said it all they did was to make faces and call me stinky and go off on their own, and they said if I went with them they'd chop my arms off, and I said I don't want to go with them anyway, because no-one would want to go with anyone so stupid as them and I wasn' scared of them, and I'd come if I wanted only I didn't." He scowled even more. "Want to play with 'em, I mean." And then he looked up at her and said with a sudden burst of confidence, "Only I did really, but I couldn' say it, could I? Not if they di'n want me. So I got nothin' to do, an' I'm fed *up*!"

"It's a problem," Isabel said sympathetically after a moment. "I can quite see it's a problem. Er – have you discussed it with your mother?"

"Her!" he said in fine disgust. "I tol' her, and she said – you know what she said? She said 'go and play with the other boys, darling' – after I tol' her what they'd said and what I said and everything! She never listens to nothin' I say. Anyway today she was goin' with rottenunclestinkyjack to get a new fur coat so she hadn't any time to talk about it."

"With *who*?" Isabel said weakly.

"Rottenunclestinkyjack" he said again and grinned. "He's her new husband and I'm s'posed to call him Uncle Jack, and I hate him because he calls me Sunny

112

Jim. So I call him rottenunclestinkyjack. Only he doesn't know. One day I'll tell him. When I'm nearly nine." And he sank again into a silence in which he mulled over the injustices of his short life, and Isabel looked down at him, and could have wept for him.

"What ideas have you had so far?" she ventured at last. "I imagine you've thought of a few things you could do this afternoon – "

"Oh, yes," he said, and now he stretched out on the hot paving stones beside her to lie with his head cushioned on his arms and squinting up at the sun. "I thought of swimmin' and I've done that. And I thought of going down to the beach and kickin' sand around only the others is down there and they'll think I've followed 'em which I wouldn't do for anythin', and I thought of mountaineerin' on the balconies only the chambermaid saw me and shrieked like a train." He giggled suddenly. "She was ever so funny. She shrieked like a train, and she waved her arms like the signals."

"I am sure she did," Isabel said absently, and then with all the delicacy she could muster – "Ah – what exactly is mountaineering on the balconies?"

"Oh, it's a game I thought of. You tie a string round your middle and you climb on one balcony and then across to the next one, and then you slide down to the underneath one and keep on till you get to the bottom."

He sighed a little sadly. "I can do it side to side but I can't do it downwards yet. Every time I want to try there's someone wavin' their arms and shouting. So I'm *fed up*."

"Uh, Fred – " Isabel said and then stopped.

"What's matter?" he squinted sideways at her.

"Uh – do me a favour, Fred, would you? Next time you think of going mountaineering, will you take me with you?"

113

"Take you? Would you come?" he said eagerly.

"Oh, yes, indeed I would! Promise me, word of honour and hope to die you'll come and get me to come with you next time you decide to go mountaineering?"

He frowned at her. "You're bein' like the others. You're not shoutin' and waving your arms yet, but you are inside your head, aren't you?" he said accusingly.

Perceptive child, she thought, and grinned at him. "Well, yes, just a bit. It's dangerous, you see. You do see, don't you?"

"Well, o' course!" he said disgustedly. "Tha's why I want to do it!"

"And that string round your waist – it's supposed to be tied to someone else at the other end, isn't it?" she said swiftly.

"Ye – es – "

"So if you let me come with you, I can be tied to the other end, can't I?" she finished triumphantly. "So we'll do it right, and then no-one can be a train and wave their arms at you because I'll be there."

After a moment a long slow smile curled over his face, and he nodded. "You're sensible. I said you was, I tol' all of 'em. All right. I'll call you first. Where will you always be?"

"Oh, you can ask them at the desk in the hall – they'll always know. I'm in the clinic most of the day, and if you come down sometime I'll show you how we do operations. You'd like that – Er, Fred, let's swear a horrible oath."

"Ooh, let's," he said enthusiastically. "What about?"

"About being blood relations that will call each other to go mountaineering. All right?"

"All right," he agreed, and held out both his hands, and she held out hers and they crooked their little fingers and crossed their wrists, and he chanted "Swear, swear,

swear" and she repeated it after him, phrase for phrase until he'd finished.

"Swear, swear, swear, cut your throat and hope to die, horrible blue in the face with your tongue sticking out, if me or you goes mountaineering without the other one. Swear, swear, swear."

"That was *very* horrible," she said approvingly as they let go each other's hands, and he grinned his gap toothed grin at her and said cheerfully, "It's my best one. Would you like some ice cream, blood relation?"

"Yes, please," she said promptly, and he jumped up and went running off towards the little bar in the corner where the barman always kept ice cream lollies for the children, and she watched him go, her face creased anxiously.

To have behaved like the average adult and shown anxiety about his fantasy of climbing the balconies – for she was pretty hopeful it was a fantasy – would have been foolish, in case he was in fact absolutely serious. Isabel had spent too long working in children's wards in the days before becoming a theatre sister not to know that. There was nothing like adult opposition to make a lonely unhappy child follow a particular course of action. Yet had she made sufficiently sure he wouldn't attempt any dangerous climbing without telling her first? She could only hope so.

As she watched him come back, carefully if indiscriminately licking the drips off the ends of both lollies, she thought, "I must talk to his mother about him. Tactfully, but she'll have to know, he's a very unhappy little boy, this one – "

"What's bright orange and comes out of the ground *voom*?" demanded Fred.

"Don't know," Isabel said after the necessary pause.

"An E-type carrot of course!" shouted Fred triumphantly.

115

And until she had to dress to return to the clinic at four she sat with Fred, and they talked and exchanged riddles and generally enjoyed each other's company.

Isabel took him with her to see the clinic when she did go, for there was still no sign of his mother and stepfather, and even though Fred had exhibited no further interest in balcony mountaineering, she wanted to take no chances.

It was almost six by the time a message came down from the desk in the foyer (for she had told them the child was with her) to say his parents had returned, and she sent him off to them with a cheerful smile and the promise of a swim with him the next day, determined that one way or another she would have to make that handsome girl with the mane of fair hair see just how unfair she was being to her small son.

And then, she finished her afternoon's work, and hurried up to change for her date with Biff, and grinned cheerfully to herself in the mirror as she did her hair. Really, life in this island was turning out to be interesting as well as great fun. The decision to spend her summer here would prove, she was quite sure, to be one of the best she'd ever made.

10

"Well, I suppose he could be an okay guy," Biff said moodily. "But for my part, he'd have to go one hell of a long way to convince me he was. After the way he behaved that night? Like some – "

"Now, Biff, please! This is my boss you're talking about, remember? He's apologized and done his best to show he means it – what more can you ask?"

"Is that all he is to you?" Biff said abruptly after a moment.

"All? How do you mean?"

"Just a boss?" He sounded a little shy suddenly. "I mean – oh, hell! It's none of my concern, really, I guess, but he – you were so mad at him when I talked to you before, and now all of a sudden it's like he was some special sort of boyfriend!"

"You're right it's none of your concern!" she said sharply and he reddened and nodded, and for a while they sat in stiff silence, staring at the people sitting round the marble topped tables and talking with a great wealth of gesticulation, and Biff twisted his sangria glass between his hands and looked miserable.

"Oh, Biff, I'm sorry!" she said at length, looking at his downcast face and feeling ashamed of her own sharp tongue. "That was very rude of me. Of course you'd a right to be interested! It was just – " she stopped and now it was her turn to look down at her glass and feel uncomfortable. "Oh, I don't know. He's being very nice to me, now, and I can't deny he's an attractive man, but as for boyfriend – oh, it's daft!" she looked up at him and smiled ruefully. "I barely know the man! I've a suspicion I'm being affected by all this Spanish romance, the whole Majorcan glamour bit – at my time of life!"

"Ach, you're just a wee bit bairn!" he said promptly with a creditable imitation of her accent that made her grin, "but a very intelligent one for a' that!" He spoke more soberly then. "If you can see that this island tends to make people a bit – oh, I dunno – over-romantic maybe, is what I mean, then you'll be okay. Too many girls come here and get swept away by some Spanish grandee type, thinking they're going to live a life of glory for ever and ever, and find out just how unglorious it is. I know – distant cousin of mine did it. They lasted six months, and now she's back home trying to get a divorce – "

"Oh, Biff, come on! We're talking about a man I've had one date with – just one date – and you're already jumping around talking about divorces! Like, do me a favour!" and at her imitation of his accent he grinned hugely, and then drained his glass and reached for the jug.

"You're great, Isabel! You're my kind of people! Come on – we'll forget it! Have another drink, and something to eat – " and he pulled towards her one of the row of flat filled dishes on the bar at which they were sitting perched on high stools. "Try this – it's local and it's great."

"What is it?" she peered into the dish, filled with blackish coloured objects in a dark heavy sauce, which smelled delectable though it looked a shade repellent.

"Calamares," he said, watching her lift a piece out with a fork, and put it in her mouth. "Good, hmm?"

He took some too and they chewed happily for a moment, and then as Isabel reached for a second piece – for it did indeed taste delightful – he added casually.

118

"Calamares – squid." "*Squid?*" she dropped the fork and almost squealed. "You mean *octopus?*"

"That's it! Cooked in its own ink – don't look like that! It tasted all right, didn't it?" He began to laugh then at the look of horror on her face. "You'd better not go to a Moorish feast anytime, honey! There they give you sheep's eyes – oh, come on! If you can eat anything as ghastly as haggis you ought to be able to manage a tender little squid without any trouble!"

"Haggis is not ghastly! It's the greatest food there is – great chieftain of the puddin' race – "

And so they went on, giggling a lot, teasing each other, eating and drinking, and eventually getting involved in a long and complex conversation with several of the Spaniards in the little bar who joined in Biff's attempts to teach Isabel more about Spanish food. She sat there surrounded by friendly happy people, with the warmth and security of Biff's solidity at her shoulder, and laughed more than she had for months. The men greeted her pert attempts at their language with great gusts of approving laughter, and Biff smiled and watched her contentedly and altogether she felt very special. Very special indeed.

As they strolled back to the hotel along the Bay-fringed Paseo Maritimo, watching the boats bobbing on the wine-dark sea ("This place!" she thought briefly. "Makes you even think in poetic quotations!") she tucked her hand into the crook of his elbow and looked up at his nice square face in the fitful light of the lamps they passed and the swooping traffic headlights. And he smiled down at her and patted her hand and they walked on companionably while she tried to find words to tell him how grateful she was.

"It's just that – I suppose you turned up at a time when I really needed a friend, you know?" she floundered. "And you really make me feel good, Biff. That I've got someone to lean on if I have to and – "

"That's great, Isabel," he said quietly. "That's – well, you couldn't have said anything that could make me feel happier." He patted her hand again. "It's a privilege to be your friend, believe me, and I want you to know that I can be leaned on any time you want. You just shout, and I'll be there, I promise."

It wasn't until they had almost reached the hotel that he spoke again, and then his voice was a little strained. "If you want to tell me to mind my own affairs again, Isabel, then you go right ahead and do it – but let me ask you just one question. And try not to be sore at me? I mean, just say you'll answer me, or say you don't want to talk about it, but still be friends?"

"That sounds very solemn!" she said lightly, looking up at him and smiling, but now his face was serious.

"Well, you got sore at me before, talking about old Fancy Pants – sorry, your boss in there – " he smiled very briefly then – "so maybe you'll get sore again:"

"I won't!" she said. "Honestly, to hear you go on, you'd think I was a bramble bush! I'm no' that prickly! So ask away, and if I don't like to answer, you can be bound I'll say so."

But when the question came, it made her stand quite still so that her hand was pulled out of his elbow's crook, and he had to turn on his heel to look at her.

"Who is Jay?"

They stood there on the pavement looking at each other as other strollers pushed curiously past them, and after a moment she said in a tight little voice, "How do you know about Jay?"

"On the plane," he said simply. "You were dreaming, you remember? And talking – calling out – I woke you."

She nodded slowly, and then started to walk again, but

120

this time she did not hold his arm. There was a long silence while she thought, while she let memories of Jay go romping uncontrolled through her mind, his face, the sound of his voice, the places they had been and the things they had done together, his kisses, his passionate demands and caresses and her own abandonment to them, and finally, the things he said when he was ending it all –

And then, with an almost physical effort of will, she pushed the memories back, downwards, collecting them and tying them and pushing them away, and shutting a door on them somewhere in the deepest recesses of her mind, and she turned her head to look at Biff, walking tensely beside her and looking down at her with his face anxiety-creased, and said quietly, "Jay was the man I was in love with. Very much in love with. We – it was a very real and complete relationship, Biff. And now it's over. He – he put an end to it. So I came here to get over the whole affair. I'm not sure what's going to be the hardest thing to get over – the way I felt about Jay, or the way my – I suppose you could call it pride – was chopped up when he said 'no more, thank you'. Either way, I'll get over it, given time."

She smiled at him then, and tucked her hand into his elbow once more. "I'll tell you this much, Biff. If it was just my pride that was hurt you gave it a splendid lift, being so friendly on the plane and being so nice now. And so of course has Sebastian Garcia, because I'd have to be a real idiot not to admit it makes a girl feel great to have nice personable men showing they think she's not so bad."

"You're not so bad," he said quietly, and his hand closed warm and strong over hers, and held on so that she felt again that sense of being specially protected. "Your Jay must have been out of his tiny mind. If I had the good fortune to be loved by a girl like you – well, you can be sure she'd never have cause to run off to get over *me*! Thank you for telling me, Isabel. I shouldn't have asked, maybe, but you said you saw me as a friend, and I thought – well, what are friends for?"

They had reached the Cadiz now, and stopped on the pavement outside for a brief moment.

"Shall I come in for a while, Isabel?" he asked, and after a second she shook her head but smiled as she did so.

"Do you mind not, Biff? Not tonight, I – oh, it's been a lovely evening, and I've so enjoyed it and laughed so much but now I want to think for a while. Just be quiet and think. Do you mind?"

"No – as long as you think of me as well as of Jay and Garcia and whoever else is in line for your company!" and she laughed and raised her face to kiss his cheek, for it seemed such a natural and happy thing to do, and he hugged her briefly and let her go very quickly.

"I'll call you tomorrow, Isabel," he said and his voice was somehow flattened. "And we'll make plans for some expeditions. Good night, my dear." And he was gone, leaving her with a warm and comfortable glow inside.

And long after she had gone to bed, to lie staring up at the ceiling with its mottled patterns of dim light reflected from the sea beyond her balcony, feeling the cool breeze that moved the curtains at her open window creeping delicately across her face, she went on thinking, but this time not about Jay alone, but about herself, and her own reactions to the men she knew, and the way her feelings would sway from side to side. And eventually she laughed softly at herself in the darkness, and turned over to curl up and fall tranquilly asleep, her last thought being a firm decision to stop thinking about herself quite so boringly much, and to remember she was here to do a job. And to get on with it.

And the decision seemed to hold. For the next two weeks

she lived happily and busily, enjoying her clinic sessions with her patients, adding to her care for cuts and bruises and aches and pains a little discreet health teaching for the chamber maids on such matters as reducing diets and personal hygiene (which seemed to amuse and fascinate them in roughly equal proportions) and dealing with the trickle of visitors who came to see her with insect bites or symptoms due to overeating and over-drinking and occasionally sunburn (for it was still too early in the season for any severe cases).

Vanda Connaught seemed to have gone into a sort of voluntary retirement, for although she was undoubtedly still in the hotel, Isabel never saw her, and heard no more about the disagreement between them.

But she saw a good deal of small Fred-Daniel on most days, for his parents seemed rarely to be in the hotel with him. They were booked to stay for a full six weeks ("*Vairy* rich, the Señor Rendell," Jaime Mendoza said in reply to her discreet inquiries about the family. "He has the factory, you understand, that makes the dresses for the cheap shops, and he makes much, much money from this") and Isabel, angered at their neglect of the child, for she felt he was missing school for far too long, set about providing him with daily entertainment that disguised some solid education in the middle of the fun.

He would sit in her office, his head bent sideways and his tongue protruding with concentration over his moving fist as he made maps, and laboriously wrote long lists of the equipment that would be needed for a safari adventure in Darkest Africa, and made graphs of the amount of mileage they would do, he and Isabel, as they made their way through the trackless Wastes Infested with Wild Ferocious Animals, a plan they discussed with great relish and at considerable length. And as long as Fred-Daniel didn't notice he was learning a good deal of arithmetic

123

and geography in the process – not to mention spelling and similar tedious matters – Isabel was content.

And her private life, too, was giving her as much interest and amusement as her working one. She rode several times with Sebastian Garcia in the foothills of the mountains, she on a quieter and darker coloured mare than Sebastian's Donna Clara, but quite lively enough an animal for her to control, and breathed the heady scent of the acres of pink and white almond blossom he showed her, billowing and shimmering in the Spring sunshine under the china blue sky like some vast expanse of candy floss. They rode for miles until she was breathless and almost numbed by the aching of her muscles, to sit peacefully in a small village bodega beside a log fire, which, surrounded by hard wooden settles with goatskins tossed across them for comfort, burned smokily in the centre of the whitewashed room. She would sit staring dreamily at the flames and sipping ice cold sherry drawn from great barrels of ancient timber, and sometimes talking a little to Sebastian, but more often just sitting and listening to him.

And she went out with Biff too, different outings entirely, when they giggled and joked a great deal, quite unlike the quiet seriousness of her expeditions with Sebastian. Biff would choose absurd fun things to do, like riding donkeys in a farmyard, and going on noisy touristy excursions where everyone sang and behaved as though they'd known her for years; none of Sebastian's slightly remote and patrician air about Biff, she would think, amused, watching him tossing a delightedly shrieking two-year-old ear-ringed moppet in the air while her stall-keeping mother filled Isabel's arms with flowers, and nodded and beamed her approval at the Americano's friendliness.

It was this contrast between the two men that made

them both seem so particularly interesting to her, she decided. Sebastian would take her in her elegant new dresses (specially made for her at incredible speed and cheapness by a little dressmaker to whom Consuelo had introduced her) to large and splendid restaurants where there were huge mirrors and acres of marble and stiffly correct venerable waiters who bowed all the time, for all the world like a setting for a turn-of-the-Century French play where she would sit in rather agreeable tension, enjoying the role of sophisticated lady in which he seemed to cast her, being quiet and elegant and a little blasé. But Biff would take her in her casual slacks and shirt to the bustling jostling street market that sprawled across the centre of Palma on Saturdays, where donkeys and chickens and rabbits in cages added their personal farmyard smells to the odours of spices and hot fried foods and fruits and vegetables that littered the pavements and would make her feel very young and giddy and giggly. With Sebastian, there was talk of books and music and plays; with Biff inconsequential chatter that meant little, but was easy and relaxed.

And as well as discovering different aspects of her own personality, as each man drew out of her the sort of response he needed, so did she learn about them. She discovered that Sebastian, for all his seeming aloofness, was in fact quite communicative about himself. He was the only son of a widow who lived quietly and very much wrapped in her religion in Valldemosa, in the mountains, and who clearly demanded – and obtained – from her son a filial duty and affection that he gave unstintingly. "La Madre" clearly figured large on Sebastian's horizon, as it did for any well-bred Spaniard.

That the family he came from was one that had once been rich and fairly powerful in a local sort of way was implied in what he didn't tell her, rather than in what he did. His calm assumption of authority, his personal success in all his dealing with other people, made it clear that there was this aristocratic streak in him, but she found it, to her surprise, quite unoffensive. Herself brought up in a tradition of sturdy independence with a healthy scorn for the effeteness of "top people" and an even healthier respect for the virtues and values of the ordinary man, she would have expected herself to be resentful of and hostile towards this calmly superior man. But somehow she wasn't, accepting him entirely at his own valuation, for always he was kind and gentle and completely punctilious. And though he still made her, quite often, feel that special internal shiver, never again did she fall into the trap of thinking he was going to make some physical overture towards her.

But Biff, for all his openness and friendliness and streams of talk and banter, in fact told her very little of himself. Within a couple of weeks she felt she had known Sebastian since his childhood, for all his remote air, but with Biff it was as though he had appeared readymade with no background at all. For he talked not at all about his family, his home, or his life in the States, sheering off into jokiness whenever she made some glancing reference that could have been construed as a question. Even about his work he said little, though she knew he worked hard during the days when he was not with her, and he somehow never seemed to notice her offhanded requests to see the building he was working on away on the Andraitx side of Palma. She found this a little puzzling at first, but then shrugged it off and forgot it; the main thing was that he was an easy friend, a delightful companion, and someone who made her feel gay and relaxed and cheerful. She asked no more.

And so it could have gone on, the weeks drifting together into months while her emotional sores healed and she became heart-whole again. It could have gone on – but it didn't.

She came cheerfully down to breakfast that bright and shining morning in late March, whistling under her breath, and thinking pleasurably of the projected trip to some splendid caves on the far side of the island to which Biff had promised to take her that evening, and as she went towards the restaurant and her morning ensaimadas and orange juice, Jaime Mendoza called her name.

"Isabella! Please to wait – I have here for you some post. I would have sent it to your room, but I thought if I saw you I give it you myself!" He came bustling across the hallway towards her, holding out a letter, a long white envelope spattered with stamps.

She frowned for a brief moment; who would write to her? She had quite deliberately not given her address to any of her friends at the Royal, wanting only to cut herself right away from the place and its memories, at least for this summer; and her cousin Fiona who was the only relation she had left since her father's death and with whom she had left her Spanish address in case of emergencies was far too busy with her own life and husband and children to start writing letters just for the sake of it. Unless something was wrong with one of her family Isabel thought and for a moment her heart sank. Although Fiona was not a very close relation, she was all the relations she had, and Isabel put her hand forwards with a sense of sudden dread.

"Letters from home are always good to have, verdad?" Mendoza said busily, peering interestedly into her face as she looked down at the thick white envelope. "Perhaps you ask some of your people to come from Scotland to visit us? Now you are such good friends with Señor Garcia – " and here he leered a little " – perhaps he can arrange the special terms for them, hey? This would be very nice for you – "

But she let the sound of his voice run on over her head, not hearing a word. For the handwriting on the envelope was not Fiona's neat and boxy script, but the untidy sprawling scribble that she knew so well, and had thought she would never see again.

Jay had written to her.

11

The letter, unopened, sat against her hip inside her uniform pocket, burning its imprint against her skin, and yet she left it there. She ate her breakfast mechanically but drank more coffee than she usually did. She prepared her clinic, and then dealt with her patients, giving them her bright smiles and interest and correct and careful care, but showed even more concern than she usually did. She cleaned the clinic when the last patient had gone, but scrubbed and polished more thoroughly, if that were possible, than she usually did. And all the time, Jay's letter sat there inert but almost malevolently active in her hip pocket; nothing she could do would eradicate its shadow from her mind.

And at twelve thirty she was free, with no more work to interpose between herself and it, and she stood in the middle of her gleaming quiet clinic, with just the distant sound of clattering glasses from the pre-lunch drinks on the terraces and the hiss of steam from the sterilizer, and turned the envelope between her fingers. For a long moment she stood there, feeling extraordinarily tense, almost as though she were on a stage and waiting for the moment when the curtain would rise to reveal a vast audience waiting for her; and then with a jerky movement she thrust her thumb under the flap and ripped it open.

And at that moment the door opened, and Fred was standing there, his tanned face serious under his sunbleached thatch of hair, glowering at her, his mouth set in the mulish lines he could so easily produce.

"Isabel!" he said loudly, and his voice seemed to jar on her as it never had, for she was filled now with a desperate urgency, a need to pull the folded sheets from the envelope and smooth them out and devour with her eyes the sprawling words. "Do you know what rottenunclestinkyjack has done now? Do you know what? And her, she says it too, an' all, and – "

"Look, Fred. Please – not now – I'm rather busy and – "

He frowned. "No you're not," he said flatly. "The waitin' room's empty an' there's no one in here. An'! – "

"I tell you I *am*!" she snapped, feeling every atom of her body stretched and twanging like a guitar string. "I'm – I have things to think about. Not now, Fred, please. Later – come down after lunch. Then. Not now – " and her fingers twitched on the envelope with irritation.

The child stared at her for a long moment, and then he let his lower lip thrust forwards as he looked at her, and the effect was to make him seem preternaturally wise, filled with a sharp knowingness. "You're not busy," he said again, and it came very flatly at her. "You're tellin' me to go away an' play an' stop bothering you, that's what you're really saying."

"All right! That's what I'm really saying!" she said, and her own voice was loud and irritable, and she knew it. "I've – I've things on my mind right now, Fred. Please, come back after lunch."

"It's important," he said, still not moving and now her temper almost overcame her and she moved forwards briskly, and putting her hand on his shoulder turned him crisply about and held the door wide open for him.

"Nothing's so important that it can't wait till after

130

lunch," she said firmly. "Now, get away with you, and I'll talk to you about it then, whatever it is."

He went without any further demur, looking over his shoulder at her just once as he went through the door. Then, his very blue eyes hooded as he looked down, and he went stumping purposefully across the waiting room and away, and she closed the door with a sharp snap and went back to the table in the middle of the clinic room to lean on it and try to stop her trembling. For now she *was* trembling, and she knew the control she had been holding so iron-strong all morning had broken, and it was reaction triggered by her irritation with the child that had broken it.

"I shouldn't have been so snappy," she thought briefly, as with shaking fingers she pulled the letter from the envelope, and unfolded it. "I'll have to apologize and try to explain why after lunch – "

But at the first sight of the words on the page, her concern about Fred was washed quite away; she forgot him immediately. "Bel-beloved" she read.

Bel-beloved. A very special name he had used for her on the very first time they had made love. They had been on a picnic by the river, near Richmond, and he'd brought a half bottle of wine and chicken pies, and they had eaten and drunk and talked a little shyly, for they had known each other only a very short time, after all, and then, there in the long summery softness of the grass he had quite suddenly leaned forwards and taken hold of her very roughly and urgently and kissed her till she was breathless, had pulled her down beside him into the hidden-away circle of waving grass stems, and had kissed her more, had caressed her ever more urgently until she felt she was no longer herself, no longer Isabel, the cool, the sensible, the sometimes dour Isabel, but part of him, the other half of herself found in him, and she had responded with an

131

urgency of her own that startled her even as she knew it was right and good and real. And later, much later, they had lain side by side, breathless and almost stunned with surprise at themselves, staring up at the cloudiness of an English June sky, and he had murmured, "Isabel – my Bel – Bel – beloved."

And so it had been ever after. Whenever they were alone together, whenever they melted into each other as they had that afternoon by the river, he had said it. Bel-beloved.

And now she stood in a room filled with glittering chrome and glass, in the alien sunshine of a foreign country hundreds upon hundreds of miles away from him, and it was as though he were there beside her and she could smell the special rich smell that was him, ether and anaesthetic and tobacco and clean human skin, the essential maleness of him, and she felt her muscles shake with a need for him. Just at the sight of two words written in scrawled black ink.

"Bel-beloved. I think I was wrong. Not wrong to tell you there was no future for you with me, not wrong to send you away for your own sake, for that still holds – I know it does. I'll never be to you what you want and deserve – a virtuous and faithful husband, a father to the children you'd like to have. That still holds. But I was wrong to myself. I should have gone on being the selfish bastard I always have been, and stopped myself from thinking about you. I should have let you go on as we were, and enjoyed being with you as long as you were willing to stay on my selfish terms. I don't know why I'm writing this letter, not really. But I miss you quite horribly. I'd be a liar to pretend I haven't spent some time with other girls – I have. People you know. And do you know something? I chose them *because* you know them. Right now I'm sitting here in my room feeling like hell, and Bar Haydon has just gone storming out in a rage because I tried to make love to her but forgot myself and called her by your name. And she is not going to be a substitute for you, she said, and I'm twenty kinds of a bloody fool if I don't go out there to that damned hotel and marry you out of hand – oh, hell, I don't suppose I'll ever post this stupid screed, not unless I get smashed first. The silly thing is I was going to write you a quite friendly cool sort of letter, the sort you would have approved of in your distant scornful days, do you remember how you were then? I got as far as phoning Fiona for your address, and did no more. And now I sit here missing you like hell and writing a lot of maudlin nonsense instead of the cheerful bit. Oh, hell, Bel-beloved, I wish I'd been more of a bastard and kept you here. But even though I miss you so, I still don't know what it is I miss. You – or your loving. I just know I want you *here*. Jay."

Very slowly she folded the pages, and put them back in the envelope, and then put the envelope in her pocket, and stood there for a long time, her hands folded on her uniform front, her head bent so that her eyes were fixed on the terrazzo of the floor. But she wasn't seeing the floor. She could see only Jay's face, see him sitting there in his bed sitting room in the doctors' quarters at the Royal, sitting at the cluttered desk with his head bent over his hand flying over the paper. She could see too, for one fleeting moment, Barbara Haydon, one of the girls she had trained with and who had become Out Patient Sister when Isabel herself had been appointed to the operating theatres; tall slender Barbara with her cheeky grin and her relaxed and easy way. Some said too easy, for there was no doubt that Bar went from one doctor to another in the Royal, seeming to fall out of love as simply and uncomplicatedly as she fell into it, shrugging away the end of each affair with a gaiety that Isabel had sickly envied in

133

the harsh days when she was fighting so hard with Jay to make him change his mind –

And now, Jay had changed his mind. Or had he? She thought of Barbara in his arms as she herself had once been, and closed her eyes sharply, trying to eliminate the image. What had the letter said after all? Not that he loved her, not that he saw her, as she once had seen him, as an ineradicable part of his future, the missing part of himself. That had been how Isabel had felt, what she had needed to tell him. And in telling him had terrified him away, for so he had told her with a desperate honesty. That he wanted her and needed her and yearned for her was undoubted; *that* she had always known. But in a physical way, only a physical way, he had cried helplessly at her. "For all I know that's all there is! All there'll ever be! You're the most exciting and devastating and marvellous woman I've ever made love with, but what you're wanting back from me is what you're feeling, and it's more than just physical, isn't it?" And she had said yes, it was more than just physical, for so it was. She loved him wholly and helplessly and all the time; and whether they made love or not didn't really matter sometimes –

And now what was he saying in this letter, which was so typical of him, so impulsive, so urgent, and – she had, painfully, to admit it – so honest? Not once had he said in the letter that he loved her, for now he used the word more circumspectly than he once had; she could recognize that. He wanted her, missed her, ached for her perhaps. But that was all.

"He doesn't know what love is," she thought bleakly. Any more, perhaps, than she did herself. What was it, after all? An aching need for another person's physical presence, a sense of the rightness and goodness that came when they were making love? Perhaps that *was* all there was to it, and Jay was expressing his bewilderment in

134

telling her that was all he had to give her. Maybe she was expressing an impossible dream in saying to him that that was all she wanted from him as long as she could go on giving him the love she felt, which seemed to her to be so much bigger, so much more important than his. But he had rejected that, seeing it as a cheating situation. To take more than he could give was not his way. And yet he missed her. She took that thought out of the morass and held it to her, close and warm. He missed her.

She stood there for a long time, her hands still clasped with deceptive tranquillity on her uniform front but her thoughts went round and round busily, mouselike and hectic. Knowing that the hard won peace of the past three weeks was false, that her belief that she had "got over" Jay was a totally erroneous one, should she stay any longer? Was there any point in it? Or was this only a temporary set-back, born of the shock of getting a letter from him? Would she regain her equilibrium by tomorrow or perhaps the day after that? –

The phone shrilled sharply and she jumped, feeling her pulse thump sickeningly and for a moment had to let it ring on while she regained her composure.

And when she did pick it up it was almost as though it had all happened before; a stream of excited Spanish, which she tried desperately to comprehend, and then a clatter as another voice took over; Sebastian saying crisply, "Fourth floor. At once. An emergency."

She reached for her emergency bag mechanically and ran, obscurely grateful for this episode, whatever it was, and feeling slightly guilty for that. She wished no illness or disaster on anyone, but having to deal with such an event would at least prevent her from mulling over and over again her own affairs.

"It's an ill wind that blows no-one any good – " she whispered aloud to the wall of the lift as it bore her upwards, and then giggled almost hysterically and took a deep breath to compose herself for whatever would be likely to be waiting for her. And almost automatically her mind began to check over the possibles; haemorrhage? stroke? heart attack? accident? –

The door hissed open, and Jaime Mendoza was there on the corridor waiting for her, his face white and pinched, and she felt a twinge of very real fear as she looked at him, for she had never seen him look so anxious.

And when all he said was a curt "Come – this way" and led a hurried way along the corridor towards a knot of people her tension grew. For Jaime to be as uncommunicative as this must surely mean something very dreadful had happened.

The knot of people were guests and staff, all craning their necks in an attempt to stare into one of the rooms, and they fell back, hissing a little in their excitement, as Jaime brusquely shoved them aside and made way for Isabel to follow him.

On the far side of the room, beside the open balcony door, stood the greyhaired man with the cigar – as ever – clenched between his teeth. "Rottenunclestinkyjack", she thought at once and fear began to build up more and more in her throat. Beside him stood a chambermaid, her face buried in her apron as she rocked her shoulders and howled noisily and Mr. Rendell was muttering something at her in obvious impatience, while on her other side the hotel housekeeper also talked steadily in an attempt to stop the woman's howling.

On the bed sat Daniel's mother, her face almost green in its pallor, sitting with her shoulders, hunched and her hands twisted in her lap, and on each side of her sat an older woman, both of whom Isabel recognized as hotel guests. They too were talking and murmuring, apparently attempting to get some sort of response from the girl who

136

sat there with her face half hidden by her sheet of pale hair, but she ignored them completely, simply staring into the middle distance.

Certainly the room seemed to be full of people, and for a moment Isabel was bewildered, looking about her for the patient, whoever the patient was, though she thought she knew, but then Jaime moved forwards and she followed him. He moved past Mr. Rendell, out of the door and on to the balcony, and here there were more people, one of the white jacketed hotel maintenance staff, a couple of waiters, and at the very edge of the balcony, leaning sideways over the railing, and apparently talking, was Sebastian.

The men moved apart as she came out on to the small paved area, and she felt the midday breeze warm on her face, and put her bag down on the paving stones, feeling the chill of certainty creeping from her belly across her shoulders and into her arms.

"Where is he?" she said and she knew her voice sounded hoarse and tense. "Fred-Daniel – where is he?"

Sebastian turned his head and looked at her, and there was an expression on his face that was compounded of tension and annoyance and oddly – boredom, and then he looked down again, and opened his mouth to speak, but changed his mind, and straightened himself and stood upright, dusting his hands with a characteristic fastidiousness.

"He is down there," he said shortly. "And will not move. If anyone makes a move for him, he says he will jump. He will talk to no one, he says, we are all to go away. But when I asked him if he would talk to you he did not refuse. So – " and he stood back, and she nodded shakily and stepped forwards to look over the balcony.

Below her the remaining floors' balconies and the hotel terraces dropped away to the water of the Bay, with the same foreshortening effect she could see from high up on her own floor, though from here it was of course less pronounced. She could see the great expanse of glass that was the restaurant roof, with waiters and guests clustered in groups and staring upwards, waving and gesticulating, and she bit her lip, for the roof looked so very large, so very fragile, and was so very much in a direct line from the balcony where she stood.

And then she shifted her gaze, to look immediately below her. She was aware of the corresponding balcony of the floor beneath, with a woman in a swimsuit standing on it and staring upwards, but she paid no attention to her, for between that lower balcony and the one on which she was herself was the narrow ledge that ran right round the building, between each set of balconies. And on it, his back to the wall and his feet planted carefully apart stood Daniel.

He was standing very firmly, she thought at first, with his shoulders hard against the wall, and his arms spread wide, the palms of his hands flattened against the wall, too. But then she saw the whiteness of his face, the pinched look round his mouth, and the faint trembling of his shoulders and she thought "He's scared – and he's tired. He can't stand there much longer – " and she turned her head and said softly to Sebastian "How long?"

He shrugged. "I don't know. The woman was looking after him – the chambermaid – she is hysterical, I can get no sense from her, perhaps half an hour – "

"Ye Gods – half an hour!" She leaned over the edge of the balcony then, and speaking very softly and almost conversationally she said "You are rotten, Fred. You promised to tell me when you were going mountaineering. And you didn't."

His head moved slowly, and then he looked up, and his eyes blazed blue in his face, so white was it under its veneer of golden tan, and he looked at her for a long moment.

"You tol' me to go away," he said flatly, and level though his voice was she could hear the panic behind it.

"You're right, Fred, I did. I'll explain about that in a minute. Thing now is, to get you up – or down. Got that string round your middle?"

"No. Didn't need it – wasn't takin' anyone else with me."

She felt the hurt anger in his voice and it made her wince. "All right, no string. So, someone'll have to come down with some – a rope – "

"No!" He spoke sharply, his voice coming loud and clear and he jerked his head up to stare at her with such malevolence in his face that again she recoiled. "Don't want to. I'll do it on my own. Or I'll fly, that's what – " and he stared down again, and even from her high vantage point, she could see the lower lip thrust forwards, and felt cold panic rising in her.

There was more to this than just a child getting into a difficult scrape and needing to be extricated; not precisely the all too common adult situation of "do-what-I-want-or-I'll-jump" but something perilously like it. A disturbed and unhappy child, not sure of anything secure in his privileged yet deprived world, playing with a fantasy of freedom and adult powerfulness –

She turned her head, looking downwards again to the roof of the restaurant below, estimating the situation. If he did fall, he wouldn't land on the balcony below but on that fragile roof, for he was just sufficiently far to one side to be in a direct line to it. Her mind moved sluggishly, as she tried, quite desperately, to think of how to behave, but somehow it did move, for she heard her own voice, speaking softly over her shoulder.

"Sebastian – send to the restaurant. Close the roof-shutters – in case he falls. Arrange for tables to be moved from the area put down – anything – mattresses, anything. Get rid of all these people – balcony below, everyone – Then go down to the balcony below yourself – catch him – "

She leaned over the balcony railing again as Sebastian moved swiftly away from her, and started to talk again to the child below, trying to find words that would reach him, that would make him feel safe and wanted and important.

"Fred, I was a very stupid person to you this morning, and you're right to be so mad at me. Thing was I had a problem. You know how it is – people do things to you that make you feel bad, make you do things you don't usually do. I'd had a letter from someone like that. It made me be a different person for a little while – "

"I came to tell you what they'd done," he said after a moment still staring downwards. She could see his hair moving gently on his forehead as the breeze lifted it, and wanted very much to be able to put her hand out and touch him, so lonely and vulnerable and helpless on his ledge. It was a physical state he was in now, but suddenly she could see that this was how it always was for Daniel. In his relationships with the adults in his life always he was poised on the edge of disaster, never able to know for sure whether he would be safe, or whether he would fall, or whether it would be quicker and easier just to fly away altogether –

"What had they done?" she said, and her voice was as light and conversational as she could make it.

"Said I wasn't to come down to you no more, not ever, because it was unhealthy with all those germs about you and wasn't to be bothered any more, and I had to stay with that woman – that maid – only she didn't talk any English – but I got away from her and I came to tell you and you said go away and play – "

"I know. I told you why. Can you forgive me? I didn't mean it. It was because – I was unhappy about a letter."

He looked up then and she could see the tremor in his neck and shoulders more clearly, for his fatigue was growing. "Are you gettin' divorced too then?"

"I'm not married, Fred, so I can't get divorced," she said gently, and became aware of movement on the balcony below, and hoped Fred wouldn't look down and see it too.

"Well, whatever it is when you get all crying all the time and angry, because of letters and phone calls. *She*'s always doin' it – not now because she only just got married to rottenunclestinkyjack but she'll do it again soon – "

He moved suddenly, apparently trying to raise his arm to rub his face, for he wrinkled his nose as the breeze blew his hair across his forehead again, and the movement seemed to alter his balance for he swayed, and went even whiter, and shrank back against the wall, peering downwards, and involuntarily she put her hand out towards him and said crisply "It's all right, Fred. We'll get you down – "

"I don't want you to!" His voice rose shrilly again. "I don't want to do nothing! I'm going to fly away, and never talk to any of you again – that's what I'm going to do – "

In a curious way she knew he was enjoying himself. The fear, the fatigue, the power he felt behind all he did and said; she knew somehow that he was aware of all this, and was enjoying it, and her fear grew; for while he still found such an element of fantasy in the whole situation, his danger was very real. If only he were too frightened to move, it would be possible to pluck him from his perch; but

141

while he reacted as he did, he could frustrate any attempt to get to him –

Far below her she saw the green shutters creep up the restaurant roof, and then she saw on the balcony below Sebastian with two men, and they were rigging up some sort of escape system – putting a long ladder across the side railings of the balcony, and she realized what he was trying to do, as one of the men – a big square-shouldered gardener – leaned all his weight on the opposite side, and another, much younger and slighter, began to creep on his belly along it towards the end that was now almost below the ledge where Daniel stood clinging to the sheer wall.

He saw them at the same moment she did, and slid his hands down the wall and forwards, and shouted – "No! – No!"

And then, inevitably, it happened. He toppled forwards, and it was almost like a slow motion cinema film for she sat there helplessly and watched the small body lurch forwards, curl up, twist, saw the hands come out with the fingers convulsively curled.

And then, incredibly, he was clinging with both hands to the last rung of the ladder, which was just below him, his small body swinging from it like a monkey-on-a-stick toy she had had once long ago in her own childhood, and the man who had been crawling along the ladder tumbled off on to the balcony as the metal structure twisted and lurched.

"We've got him now!" she thought triumphantly, and slid sideways off the railing, meaning to run back through the room and down, to get to Fred and hold him and comfort him, and make him well, somehow. And then stopped, sick and hopeless in her horror. For the heavy man on the far side of the ladder moved, as the sides of it twisted, and she could see his face crease with pain as the point of one support dug into his belly; saw him react with the inevitable reflex, let go his grip of the ladder to clutch his belly, and his own face smoothed with horror as he realized, too late, what he had done.

He reached forwards convulsively, trying to catch the moving ladder, and so did Sebastian and the thin man who scrambled to his feet from the paving stones, but none of them moved fast enough, for the ladder tipped, tilted, and rose at the far end as the lower end, with Daniel still clinging desperately, tipped over the edge and slid away and downwards. And she watched helpless and numb as the small figure lurched through the air, hit the glass roof with the ladder following, and disappeared from sight in a welter of glass fragments and noise.

12

She never knew how she got there. One moment she saw him disappear through the glass roof, and then there was a hiatus filled with shouts and jostling people and movement and fear. And then she was there, on the floor of the restaurant, looking down on the crumpled shape beneath the debris.

She realized with one corner of her mind that she had been pushed into the role of controller, for when she looked at the crowd of people clustering round him, they just stared anxiously back at her, waiting to be told what to do, and she moved crisply, kneeling down beside him.

He lay ominously still, and she said "One of you – take the end of this – only move it when I say – " and her voice was harsh and cracked. Obediently, one of the waiters came hurrying forwards, and then another as she pointed, and yet another, until, directing them partly by pointing and nodding, occasionally with a word or two, she had helped them very carefully lift off the pieces of broken metal and the great shards of glistening broken glass that were heaped over and around him.

She saw now that there were mattresses strewn about, that Sebastian had moved fast with his instructions, for Fred had landed on the edge of one, with only one small brown arm in contact with the bare floor.

And then, the glass and metal were gone, and she could see him more easily. He was lying crumpled, his head thrown back, and she looked at his face for one frightened second, at the whiteness of it, the way the eyes were rolled back and half open, and was filled with the sick certainty that he was dead. And put her hand out and touched his wrist, and fumbled her fingers urgently, and then there it was. The thin reedy movement of his pulse.

Now she moved more swiftly, checking his mouth, pulling his lax jaw forwards so that his tongue was raised, and he gasped and moved slightly and she wanted to shout, but all her training reared up and restrained her, and she said in a quiet controlled voice "He's alive."

Somewhere behind her there was a sound, a sort of rough sighing, and she turned her head briefly to look. Mrs. Rendell was leaning against one of the women, and her face too was white, and her eyes rolled back so that for a moment she looked incredibly like the small figure on the floor. And even as Isabel looked at her she crumpled and slid downwards, and one of the men grabbed at her. And then Isabel stopped caring and turned back to the child.

Her hands moved swiftly but very carefully over his body; arms, legs, ribs; neck, shoulders, head. And under her touch he began to move restlessly, and then, sharply, to wail a high thin cry, and she stroked his cheek with one hand and murmured "All right, Fred. It's all right, you're fine – soon be fine – "

But he whined again, and then suddenly reared up and opened his eyes and stared at her, and tried to roll away from her and again she put her hands on him, this time across his shoulders, gently forcing him to lie down, and he let her push him back, but was shouting and crying quite loudly now.

"I've sent for the ambulance," Sebastian's voice said in her ear, above the noise Fred was making. "How is he, do you think?"

She laughed shakily. "It's incredible – it really is. As far as I can tell he's not much more than badly concussed. He's no broken bones so far as I can see, and he's not bleeding much – just those scratches on his legs, you see? Where he went through the glass, I think – and he'll be sure to have some bruises – but apart from that, I think he's all *right* – "

"Well, thank God for that!" A gruffer voice cut in, and she looked up and saw Mr. Rendell staring down at the boy, and she thought absurdly "He's still smoking that damned cigar – "

"Of all the damn fool things for a kid to do! Is he outa his mind or something? He's lucky not to have killed himself, the little – after this, his mother'll listen to me – "

She stared up at him, at the square grizzled face and the pugnacious jaw and said stupidly, "What did you say?"

"I said he's damned little fool!" Rendell said loudly. "Thank God he's alive, of course, but you know as well as I do it'd have been no more than his own crazy fault if he wasn't. I've told his poor mother a hundred times – "

"Mr. Rendell, don't go away!" Isabel said with a very high note in her voice, "Stay right there, will you? The ambulance is here – " for she could see the stretcher and its men coming through the hubbub at the door of the restaurant " – and Daniel needs to be in hospital fast. But after that I've something to say to you – "

They put him on the stretcher, wrapping him in blankets, and he co-operated with their movements, for Isabel spoke to him softly and he looked at her with puzzled eyes and obeyed her instructions. But when he was on the stretcher he cried out suddenly "What happened?"

"You fell, Fred. You won't remember about it because you've had a great wallop on your head," she said gently. "You'll have to go to hospital for a while to make sure you've not broken anything, but they'll be nice to you – you'll like it there."

146

"Yes," he said, and his voice was still thick with bewilderment. "I'll like it there." He rolled his head a little on the pillow as the stretcher men picked him up, and then opened his eyes wide at her, and they had that same blazing blueness that had been so vivid up there on the ledge below the balcony. "Don't let them go without you. I want – I want – " and again he looked puzzled and closed his eyes and creased his forehead, and murmured "I want – "

"He'll be bewildered for a while yet," she said crisply to Sebastian. "Shall I go with them to the hospital? He'll need someone he knows – "

"Of course," Sebastian said quickly. "I will send my car for you as soon as you are to return. But do not leave him until you feel it is right – "

"Hey, what about the kid's mother – what about – er – Mrs. Rendell?" The cigar came thrusting between them, and Isabel stared at him for a long moment and then, luxuriously let go. She knew the people around her were staring and listening, that Sebastian was standing there at her shoulder, and still she said all she wanted to, releasing all the anger and tension and fear with which she had been filled.

"Daniel's mother? That – your wife? I don't care *what* happens to her! You and she between you made this child's life a hell, and by your own neglect – yes, *your* neglect, made this whole thing happen and you expect me to give a tuppenny damn about her? She can fry in hell for all I care, d'you hear me? She and you together! If you'd pushed that child out of the window yourselves, you couldn't be more guilty – and if he's alive it's no thanks to her or you! You're not *fit*, either of you, to have anything to do with any child, and as far as I'm concerned you're not worth the space you take up on this earth – now get the hell out of my way! I'm taking this child to hospital – because the poor little devil

147

needs someone with him who cares about him, and that's not *you*, not either of you, by any road – "

And she turned and pushed her way through the crowd to follow the stretcher, now bobbing its way towards the door, and then for one brief moment stopped. For, standing on the other side of her, where she clearly had heard every word Isabel had said, was Daniel's mother, and her face looked ten years older, so lined and stricken and agonized was it; and Isabel stared at her for a long moment, and knew her expression was filled with sick scorn, and didn't care in the least. She just flicked her eyes away and hurried off after the stretcher, to follow it to the ambulance and sit beside the restless child, holding his hands protectively as the siren shrieked a path for them to the hospital. Someone gave her a sandwich and some coffee – one of the nuns – and she took it gratefully, nodding and smiling her appreciation and the nun went rustling serenely away, leaving her sitting there watching him.

He lay still and quiet in the very middle of the high white bed, sleeping heavily and snoring a little, but he looked better now, tired still, but not so frighteningly white. It had been Doctor Castillo who had looked after Fred, and although they were unable to speak to each other, at least he knew her, and approved of her, and was willing to tell her all she wanted to know. And, through a very young nun who acted as interpreter, he assured her that Fred's X-rays were all clear, that he had a most miraculous escape, thanks be to the good God, and had, as she had suspected, simply a case of concussion. He would need to stay in the hospital for a day or two to insure no ill effects further, but after that all would be well.

And they had tucked him into bed, and let her stay with him for she had promised him she wouldn't go, just yet awhile, and also thought he needed time to get used to seeing nuns being nurses. So, she sat in the little private room into which they had put him and sipped her coffee and let the thoughts come rushing, for she could hold them back no longer.

She had spoken outrageously to Mr. Rendell and she regretted that – not that she gave a damn for the man, but because his wife had heard her. And Isabel knew now certainly that for all her apparent disregard of her child's welfare, and for all her patent mismanagement of his needs, she did care for him quite desperately. Isabel could see that stricken little face still, the lines that had etched themselves round the mouth, and hated herself for her cruelty. The girl was herself little more than a child; a spoiled one perhaps, but a child all the same. "Not much older than I am" she thought bleakly "but without the years of nursing I've had to sharpen my mind – and my tongue, damn it all – "

She tried to push the thoughts away again, but still they came, and couldn't be denied; for she knew with the same sureness, why she had attacked Rendell so angrily, what it was she was really saying in that fishwife outburst she had produced. She knew, as certainly as she knew her own name, that the guilt was her own. If she hadn't sent Fred away so peremptorily when he came to her in his distress, had interceded for him as he had – justly – expected her to do; if she had warned his parents as soon as she knew he was liable to go "balcony moutaineering" instead of putting it off time and again as she had; if, if, if.

She moved restlessly in her chair, and the child moved too, opening his eyes, and staring round the room, firstly blankly, and then with a sudden look of fear, and he tried to sit up and immediately she was on her feet and standing beside him.

"No, Fred, love. No – you aren't well, darling. You fell

149

on your head, and you aren't well. You're in hospital, and I'm here – Isabel – remember?"

He stared up at her unrecognizingly for a moment, and then his face cleared, and murmured. "Yes. I fell – " and then he closed his eyes again, and said very loudly "Where's Mummy? I want Mummy – "

"I – she's at the hotel, darling. She had a bad fright when you fell, and she – she's resting to get over it – " Isabel said, but he must have heard the hesitancy in her voice, for he stared at her, snapping those incredible blue eyes wide open, and his voice rose urgently. "Where is she? Tell her to come here at once! Tell her I want her – Mummy!" and this time he shouted it, angry and peremptory, and she nodded and said quickly "All right, Fred. I'll phone her – "

He looked up at her then, his face creased and suspicious. "My name's Daniel," he said after a moment. "I'm Daniel."

And she smiled and touched his cheek, and said softly, "Yes, I know. I was only joking – will you lie quietly while I go and phone?"

He closed his eyes again, and sighed a little roughly, and she stood for a moment and watched him, and saw him slide back into sleep, and moving softly, went out of the room.

Jaime Mendoza answered the call she put through to the Cadiz, "Señora Rendell? Yes – yes – I call her, at once. She is sitting here in the lounges with many of the guests – all of them, talk, talk, talk – she looks very tired of it. I fetch her – the child, he is? – "

"Fine – he's going to be fine. But he wants her – tell her, will you, Jaime?"

There was a long silence, and she stood there in the hallway of the small hospital holding the phone to her ear and watching the nuns and the doctors bustling about, the mothers with their children in pushchairs and black-shawled old ladies shuffling through, and thought "Hospitals – all the same, wherever you go. Same smells, same feeling of rush and bustle, same patients, same staff, same problems – " and then she heard the faint hiss as someone at the other end of the line breathed in, and she pulled herself back to the here and now, realizing she was quite desperately tired, and not really thinking at all clearly.

"Mrs. Rendell?" she said quickly, and there was a pause, and then a husky voice at the other end of the line.

"Yes. Yes, this is she – "

"He is all right, my dear," Isabel said, and felt the knot of guilt and anger that had lain in her belly all afternoon begin to melt. "He's all right – just concussion. He's been lucky. We both have, you and I, because – I'm so sorry, Mrs. Rendell. I shouldn't have said the things I said to your husband, but I was angry with myself because it was partly my fault – he came to speak to me and I brushed him off – and he – well, I was angry. I'm sorry."

"But you were right," the husky little voice came thinly to her, and she could suddenly see her, standing there in the telephone kiosk at the Cadiz, her hair falling heavily over her face, her head bent. "I've – I treated Daniel the way they treated me once – I forgot, you see. And I wanted – oh, I don't know. I'm – I want to see him so much. He – will he let me come to see him? Will you ask him for me?" and the pleading note in her voice was so clear, and such an echo of Daniel's own voice that tears sharply pricked behind Isabel's eyelids, and she had to take a deep breath before she could answer.

"He's asked for you. That's why I'm calling. He wants you very much. He isn't Fred any more. He's just Daniel – "

There was an odd sound, half laugh, half tears, and then the husky voice said "I should have known what it meant, shouldn't I? I should have known – I'll come now – Señor Garcia said he'd bring me – I'll come now – "

"Won't your husband bring you?" Isabel said it involuntarily and then could have bitten off her tongue, for there was a silence at the other end of the phone, so thick and heavy that it seemed to ring bells in her head.

"No, not him. I – he isn't my husband yet. He was going to be, but – well, anyway. Señor Garcia said he'll bring me. I won't be long, tell him I won't be long – "

She went back to sit beside Daniel's bed and wait and as she sat there, one hand lightly resting on the curled fist on the counterpane, the picture fell neatly into place in her mind. The girl's intense anxious absorption in the man, his aggressive posturing possessiveness, his resentment of the boy, and above all the boy's resentment of him; it all made a much more logical pattern now, and she could have wept for both of them. The lonely girl, and her lonelier child, both looking desperately for love from someone, anyone – from Rendell for the girl, from herself for the boy – when all the time there were the two of them, needing to find each other, but not quite able to –

Sebastian brought her in, and she walked straight past Isabel, giving her only one long grave glance from her wide blue eyes, as blue as Daniel's own, and then she leaned over the bed and said softly "Danny – "

He moved, opened his eyes, and looked at her, his brows furrowed, and then he smiled his huge gap-toothed smile and put his arms up and she took his hands and linked them behind her neck, and said "Hallo – "

And he murmured "Funny Mummy – " and closed his eyes again, and she twisted herself so that she was sitting beside him on the bed, and his head with its thatch of yellow hair was thrust happily against the

152

curve of her body, and she could let her hand rest gently on his.

"We'll go home tomorrow or the next day, Dandini," she said softly. "Shall we? Back to London? Just us?"

He opened his eyes sleepily again. "Just us?"

"Yes. Promise. This time I promise. Just us – "

Sebastian put his hand on Isabel's elbow and she looked round, momentarily startled, and then nodded, and together they went towards the door.

She looked up just once as they reached it, and gazed at Isabel, and then smiled, a strained polite and uncommunicative little smile.

"Er – Nurse Cameron – thank you. You've been most kind, to both of us. We do appreciate it – " and she looked down at Daniel again, dismissing everyone from the tight circle of their relationship, and Isabel nodded and said formally "Not at all. I do hope all goes well for you both – "

And then she was outside the door, and Sebastian was standing beside her, his hand still on her elbow, and looking gravely down at her.

"So now you know what nursing's all about, Sebastian!" she said with an attempt at gaiety. "Love 'em and leave 'em – patients come and patients go, and we go on for ever – "

"You are distressed," he said flatly, and she shrugged her shoulders a little as they walked together along the corridor towards the hospital entrance.

"I suppose I am – more than I should be. I let myself get emotionally involved with a patient, and you should never do that. I suppose – well, he didn't seem like a patient. Not here, at the Cadiz. Of course he was, but I let my guard down. I should have known better."

"And now you are rejected, yes?" His car was standing outside and she was momentarily startled as she realized

153

that the light was beginning to drain out of the sky. It was early evening now, and the whole afternoon had gone, so quickly.

"I suppose, so, again!" she let him hand her into the car, and he came round and settled himself beside her, lifting his chin at the chauffeur in his imperious signal, and the car purred into life. "Not that I should feel so – it's his mother he needs, not me, after all – "

He laughed then, gently, and said "And perhaps you need the children of your own, verdad?" and she suddenly reddened and he laughed again, softly.

When they reached the hotel he led her through the lobby towards the lift and she was grateful for his company, for the guests came swarming round, asking questions eager for news of Daniel's condition, and she tried to tell them, repeating it over again "He'll be fine – concussion – just a little concussed – he's been very lucky, yes – concussion."

"I will see to it that dinner is sent to you in your room, Isabella," Sebastian said as he deposited her on her floor. "I suspect you are very tired, and in need of peace and quiet to regain yourself, yes? Tomorrow, I look forward to seeing you again. Goodnight, my dear."

And he pressed the button to close the lift door and was gone, and she rode up to her room, grateful for his perceptiveness, for she was quite desperately tired, and even more desperately in need of solitude.

She bathed and put on a comfortable dressing gown and sat on her balcony to eat the delightful dinner that Carlos brought her, watching the lights come up over the Bay, and seeing them spring into existence below her on the hotel terraces.

She could see the green glow of the restaurant roof, with the jagged edges of the broken glass showing blackly against the green shutters, and almost unwillingly was

154

a little amused; he had wasted no time, the efficient Sebastian, in making his essential repairs. The blind fixed today, and tomorrow, no doubt, the glass. Soon it would be as though Daniel's drama had never happened, as though he and his mother had never come to the Cadiz – and she sighed a little and finished her meal, and went to bed.

It wasn't until she was almost asleep that she remembered that she hadn't thought about Jay and his letter for the entire afternoon and evening. "Which must mean something" she told herself drowsily, and then fell asleep with the suddenness of an exhausted child.

13

In a way it was as though Daniel's experience had come between her awareness of Jason and her own essential self, for as the days succeeded each other and March slid into April, she found that whenever she tried to think about Jason's letter and what it really meant, all that came into her mind was the day it had arrived – and Daniel. How was he? Had there been any after effects of his concussion? Did he remember anything of what happened to him? Above all, were he and his mother now on better terms with each other?

They had flown back to London a week or so after the accident, not returning to the hotel at all. Señora Lupez, the hotel housekeeper had packed and dispatched their belongings for them, and it was as though they had never existed somehow. Almost immediately new guests were in their rooms, and everyone seemed to have forgotten them.

The entire hotel indeed seemed to change its personality week by week, for the season was now swinging into summer, and holidaymakers came thick and fast. Only Vanda Connaught among the guests remained a constant factor, and she kept herself at arms' length as far as Isabel was concerned, looking icily through her whenever they happened to meet in the restaurant or the lounges. Which suited Isabel well enough, for she felt she had enough to cope with without getting any more involved with anyone else then she had to.

For she was busy. The frequent changeover of guests meant she had more and more work to do, for now more children were arriving, and with them the inevitable rash of upset tummies, cuts and bruises and aches and pains and fevers and headaches. And she used this busyness as an excuse not to think about Jay. She wrote him a brief and colourless acknowledgment of his letter, saying merely that she would think about what he had said and would write again; and indeed she meant to – when she had thought about it. But she couldn't, not in any constructive way.

She used her off duty business as an excuse too, telling herself each time that she prepared for a date with either Biff or Sebastian that tomorrow, next week, soon, she would write that letter to Jay, would go off somewhere quiet on her own and really think. And then felt a stab of guilt. For in many ways both of them were becoming more and more important to her. Biff for his warmth and friendliness and genuine concern for her, his patent determination that wherever they went would be somewhere she would enjoy, rather than he. As long as she found pleasure in their dates, then he did, and he asked no more of her than that she should laugh with pleasure or gasp with surprise or simply be interested in the places he showed her, liking this nightclub or that restaurant, enjoying this new dish or that unusual drink.

Sebastian never asked her, as Biff did, where she would like to go, what sort of entertainment she was in the mood for; he merely arranged matters in advance, taking it for granted that she would enjoy it – and she usually did. They rode, and drove and danced, went to concerts and some private parties with his friends (all of whom treated her with a careful politeness, if no real acceptance, though she realized that the language barrier contributed to this sense of being an outsider). But even though she did not always find quite so much easy pleasure in her dates with Sebastian as she did with Biff, still she found a certain excitement in his company, found herself becoming more and more affected by him as a person.

With Sebastian she was always very conscious of being a woman, a different sort of creature; with Biff she was a friend, a companion, an equal person, but with Sebastian always she was special, feminine and for that reason important.

And so it could have gone on, April moving into May, and then June coming with its steady build-up of heat that shimmered the hotel terraces into slumbrous afternoons when even swimming was too much effort, and the only really sensible way to pass the hours after lunch was to lie stripped on the bed with the curtains closed and the air-conditioning turned up to full blast, reading and dozing. The summer seemed to stretch before her, unchanging and eternal, as predictable as each day's blazing heat. Her relationships with Biff and Sebastian had the same feel of stasis about them. Each date like the one before, no real changes at all. Neither ever attempted to make any physical approaches beyond the established pattern; Sebastian gripping her elbow sometimes, kissing her hand when they parted, always punctilious; Biff accepting her friendly kiss of farewell on his cheek each time, but never seeming to expect any more overt signs of affection.

That it didn't go on was in part due to her own behaviour, and long after she was to feel hot with embarrassment whenever she remembered how it was that the summer changed gear, when she traced back the chain of events that altered it all.

It was one Sunday late in June. Biff had hired a car, and had asked her if she would enjoy a picnic over towards Andraitx, where his development was progressing well, and she had agreed that this sounded a delightful way to spend her day off. Felipe packed a picnic for her, and at eight thirty in the morning when the sun was well up but not yet oppressively hot, she went swinging cheerfully out to the front of the Cadiz to meet him, her swimsuit as well as her picnic packed into her beach bag.

"Good morning!" she cried as she saw him, sitting there behind the wheel of the little S.E.A.T. and he grinned and leaned over to open the door for her, and she settled herself comfortably, stretching her bare sandalled legs as far as the little car would let her. "I've been looking forward to this," she told him, as he put the car into gear and sped through the thin early traffic towards the Andraitx road. "I need to get right out of the town today – "

He grinned at her, momentarily taking his eyes from the road. "Now, why, I wonder? Palma going sour on you?"

"No – not Palma. Just people. Too many silly greedy people. Yesterday – Ye Gods, what a day I had yesterday!"

"So tell me all about it. Therapy, isn't that what it's called?"

"Therapy! Huh! It's not me that needs the therapy! It's *them*. Honestly, there were three men who arrived on the overnight flights – got to the hotel about seven in the morning, you know? And would you believe it – by seven o'clock last night I had all three of them lying moaning and groaning on their beds, sunburnt to a crisp, sick from eating too much, filled to the gunwhales with brandy, and wondering why they felt so lousy! You'd think grown people'd have more sense than to ruin their holidays within less than twelve hours of getting to the place! You'd think they'd have the sense to take it easy the first few days – "

"You do sound severe! Don't be so unkind, Isabel! You're here for the whole summer – for them this is

159

the culmination of fifty weeks of hard saving, isn't that so? You can understand them trying to pack in as much as they can right from the moment they arrive!"

"Pack it in is right – you'd never believe people could eat or drink so much in so short a time! Ah well, I daresay you're right – but it happens every Saturday. Always someone whose head I have to hold before the day's out. Still, I'm being a bore. Let's forget 'em! Where exactly are we going?"

"You could never be a bore," he said, and turned his head to smile at her again and she grinned cheerfully back. "Where are we going? Well, I thought maybe I'd show you the development, and then we'd have coffee in one of the little cafes by the harbour where the fishing boats come in, and then there's a place I know – a really quiet little bay no one else ever seems to go to where we could swim and have our picnic. Would that be fun? Or have you any other ideas? We could drive farther up into the mountains, maybe and – "

"It sounds a gorgeous plan Biff – just perfect. And it'll be fascinating to see the development, too. You don't talk about your work much, you know, not usually. I feel very honoured that you should show me! Like I'm a bit more than just some girl you've made friends with?" and she looked at him sideways through her lashes and smiled rather provocatively, and knew she was doing it. She didn't know why, but quite suddenly she wanted to provoke him a little to see just how much he cared about her. Was this simply the comfortable friendship it seemed or was there more to it? And perhaps it wasn't just that she wanted to provoke him into showing how much feeling he had for her; in a way, perhaps, did she want to find out how much feeling she had for *him*?

He turned his head again and looked at her gravely for a moment, and then returned his attention to the road and said with an air of casualness that for once seemed too relaxed to be real "You could say you're more than just some girl – " and then he grinned with a flash of his usual good humour, and added " – you're Isabel – and who could imagine a world with more than one Isabel? I'm darned sure I can't! You're more than enough for this mother's son to cope with, you and your Scots severity!"

"I'm not severe!" she protested, and was grateful to him for making a joke of it; to have displayed the sort of coquettishness she had always so despised in other girls – what on earth had possessed her? And she shook herself mentally and settled to enjoy the drive, talking only in the usual bantering way they did.

The development was indeed fascinating; a series of small blocks of flats, flat-roofed and pretty, clustered round a curve of blue swimming pool with carefully planted young trees and bushes to give shade to the communal terraces, the whole tucked into a curve of valley in the foothills of the mountains in such a way that the buildings looked, for all their modernity, as though they had been there for centuries.

She said as much as they stood beside the pool, staring up at the façades of the white buildings, and he reddened with real pleasure.

"Really? Gee, Isabel, you couldn't have said anything nicer? That's just the effect I wanted! I told the Old Man – I'm always telling him – that you can make money and still produce a piece of work that's beautiful, and doesn't insult its environment – this time, I made up my mind to prove it to him – seeing he isn't around to keep coming and poking his nose in and arguing with me and the architect the way he usually does – "

"He sounds a real brute, this Old Man of yours," she said. "How long have you been working for him?"

"How long? I – well, ever since college, I guess – " he

said and now the embarrassment that was usually in his voice whenever he talked of his work was back again, and she looked at him curiously.

"Well, I would have thought that someone with the ability to produce a development that looks like this ought to be able to work for anyone he wants to – if this boss of yours is so nasty and stupid, why don't you tell him what he can do with his job? I would!"

He looked down at her and smiled, a little awkwardly. "Would you, Isabel? Well, maybe you would at that – though sometimes, circumstances – I – oh, well. I'll tell you all about it some time. Not now. It's getting a bit late and it'll be too hot soon even to swim. We'll go to the bay, shall we? There's all day to talk, after all."

They parked the car high on a cliff road a few miles along the coast from Andraitx and then he led her to a narrow path that led down through a gap in the scree at the edge of the cliff to a winding footpath that made its way between overhanging bushes and cactus to suddenly plunge into darkness as it went into what appeared to be a tunnel, and she gasped with surprise and hesitated. But he laughed and took her hand warmly into his grip and led her onwards, and after a while the darkness thinned and opened out and they were standing in a sandy-floored shallow cave that was little more than a small rock-encircled gap in the cliff foot, cool and dim against the blaze of light that came from the beach and sea beyond.

"It's like something out of a child's story!" she cried delightedly, running to the rim of the cave and staring up at the towering cliffs. "Is this the only way to get down here?"

"It surely is! That's why it's so peaceful, I guess. No one spots the path at the top – you have to be told about it by someone who was told by someone else – your actual oral

162

tradition, that's what it is! I thought you'd like it. I was shown the way by one of the children of the foreman of our building gang – "

"A compliment that – I can't imagine any child showing a grown-up person such a gem of a place unless that grown-up was very special and very nice." She smiled then as he reddened. "Come on, Biff! Admit it! The child thinks the sun shines out of your ears – isn't that it?"

"Ah, kids – you know how they are – they take notions – "

"But it isn't a notion! You *are* nice! And particularly nice to have brought me here, too. It's beautiful – can we swim?"

"But of course we can! The beach shelves perfectly here – deep enough to dive out there at the point – " he indicated the rocks that marked the eastern end of the little bay – "but shallow enough to lie in the water and fall safely asleep at the edge. Look, there's a little pile of rocks over there where I can change – you change here. Last one in's a rotten egg!"

She undressed quickly, shrugging into her newest bikini, and raced across the clean white sand of the beach, feeling the heat burning her skin, but he was already in the water by the time she got there. She saw him make a perfect skimming dive from the farthest of the rocks as she reached the edge, and then he was swimming towards her with powerful easy strokes, blowing water ahead of him like a great brown porpoise.

They played and splashed and laughed for all the world like children for whom sand and water was all they ever needed, all heaven in one place, chased each other across the beach, in and out of the rocks and back into the clear blue water until they were breathless, and then lay flat on their backs at the edge, letting the minute wavelets lap around their hot skin while they squinted up at the

163

harshly blue sky with its metallic midday glare. And then, lazily and easily they walked up the beach to the welcome shadows of their little cave.

He made her lie down on a towel and rest while he put out their picnic, adding his own bottle of wine and little jars of olives and nuts to the chicken pieces and hardboiled eggs and fruit and cheese that Felipe had supplied. They ate in a companionable silence, until the sharpness of their exercise-created hunger had lost its edge, and then pushed the food remains back in her beach bag before stretching out side by side on the cool, shadowed sand, protected by the overhang of the cliff from the heavy beat of the sun that was now giving the sea a glitter of tinsel brightness, and garnishing the beach with sparks of light as grains of quartz in the sand reflected the sun.

Inevitably, she fell asleep, lying there on the yielding softness of the cave floor, comfortably replete with food, softened by the wine they had taken, gently fatigued by the swimming and running.

And woke an hour or so later, languorous and peaceful, to find Biff at her side, his head turned so that he could look at her. He was resting his head on one hand, his elbow planted in the sand, and his face seemed so attractive, so warm and brown and affectionate that she felt a sudden lift of simple desire rise in her, and put up one hand to touch his cheek.

They stayed so for a very long moment, she touching him, and staring very directly into his eyes, and then, knowing exactly what she was doing, she raised her head and parted her lips, and shifted her gaze slowly and sensuously until she was looking not at his eyes but his mouth. It seemed to her that for one brief moment he resisted, and she lifted her chin a little higher and softened her mouth even more, and let her fingers stroke the skin of his cheek very lightly. And then, as she had meant him

164

to be, he was kissing her, gently at first but then with an urgency and a need that left her breathless.

For a while she responded, returning his kiss and his caresses with an eagerness that matched his own. Until he murmured her name, saying it slowly, lingering over each syllable as though it were a kiss. And it seemed suddenly that she could hear two voices, his and Jason's. Jason murmuring, "Bel-beloved" in a distant but vivid counterpoint. "Bel-beloved – "

It was as though she had been douched with a jet of cold water. The desire that had been lying there deep inside her like some dark and secret pool shivered and trickled away to nothing, leaving her with a sense of sick revulsion, and quite sharply she rolled over, away from his hands, so urgent on her skin, away from his warm breath on her face, and jumped to her feet to stand at the edge of the cave, rigid with self-hate.

"I – I'm so sorry, Biff. That – that was unforgivable of me. To have let you – and then to leave you like – oh, God, I'm sorry! I'm not a tease, believe me! I wasn't trying to – it just happened. I was asleep and – I'm sorry."

"There's no need to be sorry," he said after a moment, and his voice was heavy with control. "I – it was as much my fault as yours. I thought I'd be able to wait, to hold out, not to rush you. I thought, maybe she'll get over him soon, she can't go on grieving for him much longer, and then – when you lay there looking at me like that I thought, maybe she *is* over him – maybe she isn't mourning for him any more – ? You said this morning, too, didn't you, about being more to me than just some girl? and I thought – oh, hell! I should have known. I shouldn't have brought you here, shouldn't have risked it – "

She turned and looked at him, then, peering to see his face in the shadows, for her own eyes were dazzled by the sun, and she frowned and said uncertainly,

"Risked it? I – don't understand. How do you mean risk?"

"Oh, for God's sake, Isabel! Don't treat me as though I were a complete fool!" His voice was rough with anger, and she could see him now, sitting on the sand with his arms clenched round his hunched knees, his knuckles white with control, and his face white, too, under its tan. "You must surely know what I feel about you! That I was waiting to ask you to marry me – waiting until you'd forgotten that bloody Jason!"

"No – no, Biff! Don't say that! You mustn't – I never meant you to get so – oh, God, Biff, you're my *friend*. I couldn't *marry* you – not ever!" And even as she said it and heard the note of amazement in her own voice, she knew just how cruel she had been. She had been almost prepared to treat him as Jay had treated her – as a sexual object, someone to play with, to make her feel good – but no more than that. And she hated herself for it.

Silently, she stood there staring at him and he sat and stared back at her, his face tight and filled with pain. And then he grimaced and relaxed and moving awkwardly, stood up, and picked up the towel on which they had been lying to shake the sand from it before folding it with dreary neatness.

"I'm sorry," he said heavily after a moment. "I thought, maybe this time – maybe this time it'll be different. But it isn't."

"Different? I don't understand – "

"Oh. God damn it all to hell, why should you? Why the hell should you?" He threw the towel on to the ground with a violent movement that knotted the muscles across his shoulders, and then whirled and looked at her. "You don't know what it's like to be me, do you? Everybody's friend, Biff, that's me – everybody's friend! Nice guy Biff, great for swanning around with but when it comes down to it, not for real – not unless they know, of course. Then it's for real all right – *their* sort of real. But it's never mine. And this time, I hoped, I thought – oh, don't look at me like that! I'll get over it, like I always do! I'll get over it!"

"Please, Biff, don't be so angry. I know I've treated you very badly, but – I – oh, I saw you as an amusing, kind, useful sort of person – not useful in a nasty way, believe me, but someone I could trust who wouldn't make life complicated for me, who'd help me get my pride back. I – my pride took a hell of beating a while back, Biff, and when you showed you like me, it helped. But I should have thought, and realized. I suppose if I hadn't been so totally selfish, so concerned for my own feelings, I'd have realized that no man goes on seeing someone unless – unless there's some strong feeling of some sort involved. Does he?"

He looked at her, his face a little twisted, and said harshly, "No. He doesn't. Not when he's had the sort of beatings I've had – you aren't the only one to have been hurt, you know, Isabel. Not by a long shot."

She went on, not really hearing what he said, trying to be honest, trying to explain to him that it was a fault in herself rather than a lack in him that had made her behave as she had.

"I suppose I was using you to prove to myself that I was still – that a man could still want me. Which was stupid as well as cruel because I know that, anyway, don't I? Didn't he write and tell me that? What I want is to be loved for *me*, to be wanted as a person, not just as – not just the way Jay wants me. And I used you to prove something I already knew, and it was – "

"Oh, don't upset yourself, Isabel! There's no need to upset yourself! Like, I'm used to it, this sort of experience. I can take it!"

167

And this time she did listen to him, and looked at him, frowning her puzzlement, and he laughed, a hard unhappy laugh that echoed the bitterness in his voice, and said, "You wondered why I wouldn't talk much about my home and my job and the rest of it? Why I stick with my job when the Old Man makes my life such a hell with it? I'll tell you why – it won't take all that long. It's on account of the business is mine. Squires Construction – one of the biggest concerns of its kind in the world, and it's mine, near as damn it. Mine and the Old Man's. My father. My lousy father. Who's got one hell of a lot more sense in his little finger than I have in my whole stupid body – "

She shook her head, confused and almost wanting to cry, for his face was so filled with misery and she knew she had created it. "I don't understand Biff – I don't understand – "

"No, sure you don't! Why should you? Look, Isabel, so I'm in love with you, okay? I know it, and you know it, and you don't feel the same way and that's all there is to it. Just my bad luck, isn't that it? And my bad luck it isn't the first time it's happened."

He was walking about now, marching from one side of the sandy little cave to the other, his arms wrapped around his chest as though he were hugging his misery to himself, and she watched him silently, feeling herself filled with his distress.

"I've been in love before – twice before. And both times the Old Man laughed – and boy did he laugh! – it's not for real, they don't care for you, it's Squires money they want, and God knows he should have experience. Three times he married, three times he got stuck with alimony – and now he's the most suspicious – ah, hell, how can I complain about him? Wasn't he right? Every god-damned time? Because he told 'em – both of 'em, he went and told 'em that the day I married every damned

168

penny I had'd be taken away from me, that I'd be the same as any other guy looking for a job. And both times he was right, they just disappeared. All of a sudden, they just didn't feel that great love and passion any more! So this time, I thought, no more. This time no girl anywhere is going to know about my family, or the money there is. So that if someone says she loves me, it just possibly might be true – just *possibly*. And I have to go and fall for a girl who's – ah, what the hell! Forget it all. I'll get over you. Like I said, I've had experience – "

"I have never said I cared for you, Biff." Her voice sounded cool in her own ears, but she couldn't help that. "I don't talk that way. I like you – I have from the start. I found you – interesting. And if I hadn't already been – if it hadn't been for my circumstances at the time I met you, I'm thinking it's very likely I'd have – that you'd not be feeling as you do now. But I'll not be blamed for anything more than you've a right to blame me for. I behaved badly – tried to arouse you and succeeded and then backed down, and that's a hateful thing to do. But I never have said at any time anything that should let you think I mean anything more than – "

"No, I know. And I'm being unfair." He moved sharply then, and walked across the sand to come and stand in front of her, and suddenly he smiled, the same familiar and sweet smile she had become so used to, and he held out his hand.

"Isabel, forgive me. I had no right to throw all that at you. Well – maybe a little right, because yes, you *did* play a game with me, and you *did* make me think that – you made me feel pretty damned urgent for a while there. And a man can behave badly when that happens. But I'm okay now. Nothing like losing your temper to take the edge off desire, huh? I've been twenty kinds of a fool, but that doesn't mean I had to talk to you as I have. So,

169

I'll forgive you if you'll forgive me, and maybe, we'll still be friends. Maybe?"

She looked at his hand, and then, gratefully, put out her own, and solemnly they shook and then let go to stand and stare at each other. And after a moment she said in a low voice, "Thank you for accepting my apology so handsomely. And of course, if you'll – if you think you can – I mean, if it isn't going to make you feel all unhappy, then I would indeed like to go on thinking we're friends. Because I mayn't be in love with you, nor likely to be, as far as I can tell, but I do like you very much, and I'd miss you sorely if I didn't see you."

14

But although they had agreed to go on as though the episode in the little cave had never happened, it was inevitable that things should be different. They had driven back to the hotel in silence, but not one of their usual companionable silences; it had been a strained and slightly polite one broken only by their over-punctilious inquiries about each other. "Are you quite comfortable, Isabel." "Perfectly, thank you, Biff – is my bag in your way? I'm so sorry – " "Not at all – "

A horrid way to be with a friend, she had thought mournfully as he delivered her to the entrance to the Cadiz and she stood on the pavement after getting out of the car, feeling awkward as a schoolgirl on a first date. And now what? Do I just say "Good-bye and thank you for having me," or just go running in, or shake hands –

He had solved it for her by holding out his own hand and once more they shook with that slightly solemn heaviness.

"Good-bye for now, Isabel. I'm sorry the afternoon turned out as it did, but I guess – "

"I'm sorry too – so let's stick to what we agreed and forget it – " she had said swiftly, and he nodded and with one final grip of her hand, let her go and climbed back into the car to drive away without a single backwards look.

And she went wearily in to spend the evening in her room, ostensibly to wash her hair and do her nails, though she usually spent an hour or so in the hotel's hairdressing salon each week for that purpose. But she had felt she couldn't face the idea of an evening in the hotel lounges chatting to guests or swimming in the floodlit pool, much as she often did enjoy such activities in the usual way.

For the next week she had to work hard, and was grateful for the fact. As well as the over-indulgent trio of men who had so marred her Saturday, there were other guests who needed a good deal of attention to their sunburns and overladen stomachs, and in addition a very minor epidemic of gastroenteritis developed among the children and took a lot of her time, and a good deal of effort explaining to parents how to prevent more children going down with it. So when Biff called her on Tuesday and suggested a date, she could say, with complete honesty, that she was both too busy and too weary at the end of each working day, and please would he forgive her –

And when he called again on Thursday she had to say the same thing, and then he didn't call at all for a week, and she was both glad and distressed; glad not to have to face the difficulties of attempting to recreate their old easy familiarity, distressed that the rift between them should be widening, that their friendship, despite their good intentions seemed to be so damaged.

She hadn't realized just how distressed about it she was, in fact, until the end of the second week. Sebastian had asked her to go with him to a concert and then on to dine at one of Palma's more elegant restaurants and she had agreed, not with any real enthusiasm but because it was easier to go than to explain why she would rather not. And she would have preferred not to, in many ways, for somehow everything seemed more of an effort these days; less amusing, less challenging, even a little boring.

She sat in the restaurant, staring down at the wineglass

she was turning between her fingers, staring into its amber depths and thinking. Am I perhaps homesick? It was after all, a very possible reaction. Glorious as the daily sunshine was, fascinating though the foreignness of Majorca was, it hadn't the glory of a London summer's day, or the fascination of work and life at the Royal, she told herself a little sadly.

She slid into a daydream seeing herself back again in her immaculate operating theatres, dealing with the many famous surgeons who worked there, crisply organizing a day's operating lists; a far cry from the rather tedious minutiae of a summer resort hotel's clinic filled with the sillinesses of greedy holiday makers or the minor problems of the staff. She saw herself at a London party with some of the extraordinary and exciting people Jay included among his friends, and couldn't help comparing that scene with the rather dull parties Sebastian had taken her to, with their overpolite and such very well behaved guests, their careful protocol.

And she sighed softly and wondered whether perhaps she shouldn't go home to the Royal and to hell with Jason – at which her thoughts swooped, tumbled and reshaped, for her own attitude towards Jason was one of the problems she hadn't yet solved, and would undoubtedly have to solve – somehow – before she went back to the Royal.

"You are, I think, a little sad tonight, Isabel."

She almost jumped and then reddened with embarrassment. "I'm sorry, Sebastian. How rude of me to be so – so abstracted. Put it down to fatigue at the end of a long day."

He shook his head, watching her carefully under those heavy lids of his. "No, I do not think that this tristeza that I observe in you – this sadness – is in any way a part of your day of work. You are sitting there, and I watch the expressions change and move on your face, and

I tell myself, she is not quite happy, Isabella. Not entirely herself. Matters have changed for her."

She was startled, for his voice had a new quality about it, one that had never been there before, and she looked at him consideringly, trying to analyse it. And decided it was concern, real concern, and was grateful for it, for that was what she missed most about Biff, his care for her welfare. To find Sebastian showing it was very comforting. So she smiled as widely as she could, and put out a hand to touch his.

"You're kind to be so concerned," she said. "Thank you. And I'm not really sad. A little – homesick, perhaps; the Island is beautiful and I'm enjoying my job, really I am, but somehow I miss London and my old hospital – "

"This I can understand," he said gravely, and put his own hand over hers on the table. "But you are not being perfectly honest with me, Isabella. Since homesickness, were it all of your problem, would I think have shown itself before. But this is the first time I have noticed these moments of sadness in you. These past two weeks."

Once again she felt her face crimson its tell-tale message, and she bit her lip. "You're a very perceptive person, Sebastian!" she said as lightly as she could. "Maybe I have been a little – unhappy lately. I've – I've had a disagreement with Biff – Mr. Squires. And I'm a peaceable soul, and I dislike such things – "

Suddenly, she felt she wanted to talk about what had happened, to seek some other person's reassurance that she hadn't behaved as badly as she really knew she had, someone who would say gently "It wasn't your fault" and thus take the load of guilt she felt from her back. And Sebastian sat there, looking at her with that air of calm and correct yet very real concern, and there was no one else she could tell –

"I am rather sad about him," she said now, looking

down at the tablecloth, suddenly a little shy. "I treated him badly."

"I find that difficult to accept. That you might inadvertently cause a person distress – this can happen to anyone. But that you should have cause to blame yourself for any deliberate unkindness – no, for me, this is not in your character."

"You're too kind," she said, embarrassed again, and tried to pull her hand away, but he seemed unaware of the movement of her fingers, and his own hand remained heavily on hers. So she left it there.

"So, tell me of the manner in which you feel you have treated Mr. Squires in a bad way, and permit me perhaps to reassure you."

"Perceptive isn't the word, Sebastian," she said, feeling a sudden warmth for him filling her. "That's perhaps just what I *do* want. Well – oh, hell, this'll sound so *conceited* – but I can't help it. I – he fell in love with me, it seems. And I like a great daft fool, I thought he was just a friend, someone I could rely on, someone to like, but not – not *ever* – someone to love."

She was looking at Sebastian, but not really seeing his impassive face, the light glinting on the silver wings of his beard, the stillness of those dark eyes; instead, she was seeing herself and Biff in that cave, was talking to Biff about it, explaining, apologizing, not talking to Sebastian at all.

"Anyway, we went out together, and it was fun, and relaxed and so *comfortable*. Until we went for that picnic. And me – there I was, trying to get another man out of my system, and I used Biff to – oh, how can I explain exactly what happened? Just that from my behaviour, Biff thought maybe that I – that I felt for him more than I do. And then I – back pedalled – I mean, I rejected him, and hurt him quite a lot, and I don't like myself one little bit – "

There was a short silence, and then Sebastian said quietly "You love another person, and it is for this reason that you have hurt your friend Mr. Squires. For this reason that you allowed him to believe you might respond to his lovemaking – and then could not – do not look so surprised that I understand that this is the root of your embarrassment! I am after all a man, and I am not entirely without an awareness of the world and its ways! But, as I say, you rejected Mr. Squires because of your affection for another person." It was a statement rather than a question but she answered it.

"Yes. That's the only reason. I told him, maybe if I weren't already – but I am and that's all about it. I'm no' likely to get over it as easy as I thought I would – that's pretty darned clear – "

And now it was Jay she was talking to, and she shifted her gaze to stare down at the tablecloth, seeing Jay's face etched against its whiteness, and felt herself filling with the old familiar misery and sense of loss. Familiar, but not quite the same, for there was still the letter he had written, full of his own confusion and unhappiness, and maybe –

"Then I believe you behaved exactly as a lady in such a situation should, and have no cause at all to blame yourself." His voice cut sharply into her thoughts and she looked at him almost in bewilderment, for she had for one brief moment forgotten he was there.

"Thank you, Sebastian. You're very kind. I've already said that, haven't I? But it's true. And I've no right to bother you with my tedious problems when you've taken me out and brought me to so nice a restaurant – forgive me."

"There is, I assure you, nothing to forgive," he moved his hand then and released her, and beckoned imperiously to the waiter, who hurried over and in response to

176

Sebastian's peremptory signals refilled their wine glass-es.

"And now you have told me of your problem, and I have reassured you that you have behaved throughout completely as you should I hope your sadness will go, verdad?" and he lifted his glass towards her with a sudden spurt of gaiety that was so unusual in him that she felt her own cheeks crease into a smile, and let her spirits lift in response.

"I hope so too," she said, and sipped her wine, and then, making a conscious effort, pushed the tensions and questionings that had so filled her mind right away and produced a very bright smile indeed.

"This has been a splendid dinner, Sebastian. I have enjoyed it and thank you very much. But I'll tell you something – we'll have to call an end to the evening, I'm thinking. Not because I'm not enjoying your company, but because of your guests."

"My guests?"

"Indeed, yes! Three more babies showed signs of gastro-enteritis today, and I'd like to check on them before their parents settle for the night. I told them I'd be back before eleven so that I could see the babies, so I really think we ought to go. And you can hardly object now, can you? As I said, they *are* your guests!"

He beckoned the waiter for the bill, and smiled at her, his rare and warming smile.

"Tell me, why this concern for my guests? Is it because they are patients – ill people – or perhaps – a little – because they are guests of the Cadiz, and you have a concern for the good name and welfare of the hotel?"

"Oh, because of the hotel, of course!" she said gaily. "I'd feel very bad if because of my inefficiency half the hotel went down with a bug – very bad for business – but generally, to tell you the truth, I get really annoyed with the people themselves! They're the first to blame the hotel if they get ill, but most of the time, it's their own darned faults! Ah, well, I mustn't be too severe, I suppose. I've been told about that before – "

"I do not find you severe," he said as the bill came, and he signed it, and they stood up to leave. "Indeed, I find you very decente – as the French say, comme il faut. It is an agreeable quality to find in so modern a young lady as yourself," and she wanted to giggle at the quaint formality of his speech.

They strolled back to the Cadiz through the bustling streets, filled with holiday makers enjoying the cool of the summer evening, and he held her elbow in that now familiar secure grip, and she felt relaxed and comfortable with him; and then was a little annoyed with herself. "What sort of wet fish are you?" her secret little voice asked jeeringly "to always need some man to lean on? Grow up, girl, do – "

But she ignored the little voice, glad to have the comfort of his grip on her arm.

He came with her to the clinic when they reached the hotel, to collect her bag so that she could start on her rounds of the sick babies she was worried about, and then accompanied her as far as the third floor, where her first patient was.

"It would be interesting for me to come with you, to see how you look after these young guests of mine, would it not?" he said, "But I feel it would perhaps not be decente for me to do so, since I am, after all, not a person of medical background."

"Oh, indeed it wouldn't," she said and grinned at him. "And to tell you the truth, Sebastian, you would find it not so much interesting as unpleasant. A child with gastro-enteritis isn't exactly aesthetic. Poor sick bairns! I'll have all the details in my report in the morning, anyways, so you'll see then what's happening. I promise you, if I'm the least bit concerned, I'll have the babes in hospital before you can turn round, for it's not a disease I'd ever neglect. So, I'd best be away – and thanks again for a lovely evening, Sebastian – and for being so understanding when I was being very silly – " and she held her hand out to him.

"Not silly," he said, and raised her hand to his lips and kissed it. "Not silly, but very naturally feminine. It was a pleasure and a privilege to have your company and your confidence, Isabella. I thank you for it."

Once again she knew her face was pink, and she bit her lip in embarrassment, and he smiled at her, and again kissed her hand before letting it go.

"Goodnight, Señorita Isabella. Goodnight, and thank *you*. I look forward to seeing you tomorrow. Perhaps you would be so kind as to bring me your clinic report at the end of the morning, if you have been able to prepare it by then, instead of giving it to Mendoza? I will by then have, I think, another matter to discuss with you."

And he was gone, leaving her feeling not a little comforted by his ready understanding of her uneasiness about Biff, and more than a little grateful, for she felt better about it all than she had since it had happened. Somehow he had helped her to put it all into perspective, and she smiled to herself as she knocked on the door of her first infant patient's room. Nice man, after all! Not a bit disagreeable as she had thought him on their first meeting. And with his care for the forms and styles of life, almost as amusing as funny little Jaime Mendoza. Nice people, the people of the Cadiz, to treat her as they did, she thought, and then went in to look at the baby sleeping in its cot by the window. Nice people, nice job. I do feel better!

15

They had gone through the clinic report together, in an atmosphere of professional yet relaxed camaraderie that was so very reminiscent of her working life at the Royal that her sense of contentment, still lingering from the previous evening, strengthened and thickened to make her feel even more sure that after all, the remainder of her summer at the Cadiz could be really enjoyable, and not just a stint to be worked through as she had begun to suspect might be the case.

And then, when she had finished telling him of the minor accidents involving the staff, and accounted for the drugs and medicines she had given the guests (all of which had to be paid for by them, since the hotel could not be expected to foot that bill) he walked across his office to bring from a wall cupboard a cut glass decanter of very pale amontillado sherry and a pair of beautifully etched glasses.

"I think perhaps we have el aperitivo, yes? This sherry is brought for me especially all the way from the cellar of a friend of mine in Barcelona where he matures and cares for the most remarkable wines. You will, I think, like it. Salud!"

They sipped their sherry in peaceful quietness for a while, and then he stirred in his big chair and put his glass down with very neat precision, and leaned forwards to fold his hands on the desk before him.

"You will recall that I said last night that this morning, I would perhaps have another matter to talk of with you, and this is now so," he said, and she raised her eyebrows at him, for he sounded even more precise and formal than usual if that were possible.

"I wish to take you to visit Valldemosa with me on Sunday next, Isabella. This is a place, I think, you have not yet been to – "

She shook her head. "Not yet – though I've heard a good deal about it. It's the village where Chopin and George Sand lived for a while, isn't it? Very romantic and beautiful, that story."

He shrugged slightly. "Perhaps a little too romantic for good taste. For myself I find it all a little – sordid, is I think the word. All a matter of commercial exploitation. As a business man I am of course not opposed to good business matters, but the very commercial use of the Valldemosa legend is one I find a little unpleasant. However, our visit to Valldemosa is not concerned with the exploits of musicians or the later moneymaking that such exploits lead to – "

She felt her lips quirk, and bent her head for fear he should see it, for she would not hurt his feelings for the world. But he was so very funny, sounding more like a character from a nineteenth century novel than a real person.

Clearly he had not noticed her glint of amusement, for he was still talking with the same somewhat stilted air. " – Our visit is for more personal causes. Valldemosa is my family home, you understand. I of course live most of my time here at the Cadiz, now that I have to be so concerned with the running of the hotel, but always, for home, I think of Valldemosa."

He stopped and she smiled encouragingly at him, and sipped her sherry, and felt herself warming to him even

181

more, remembering with a sharp wave of nostalgia how she felt about Scotland; for although most of her adult life had been spent in London, still the soft greenish-blue hills and moors of her Scottish village home were very precious to her, and she knew what it was that Sebastian felt for his home in Valldemosa, and would always feel, however long he lived and worked in Palma.

"So," he was saying. "On Sunday I would like to take you to see my home, and to meet my mother. She, of course, still lives there, and I visit her at regular intervals. Tell me, you are willing to come with me to meet her?"

He looked at her with his head on one side, watchful and expectant and she finished her sherry, and smiled again at him, and said warmly, "I'd like to very much. It's most kind of you to ask me. Thank you."

"It is, you understand a visit of some formality – my mother is an old lady of very definite – ah – ideas, you understand. She is the daughter of a family of great antiquity and honour, and as the wife of a son of a family of equal position, she has lived her long years according to many rules. To some people she seems particularly old fashioned. But I do not, for one, feel that being old fashioned is always so bad a thing."

"Oh, I agree! And of course I understand! I promise you I will be very what was that phrase? – I can't remember – anyway, I'll be as correct and polite as I know how to be. I'll not let you down."

She smiled again, a little wickedly this time. "And since it was your mother's idea that I should be here at all – that the Cadiz should have its own clinic, then it's only right and proper she should have a chance to have a look at me, don't you think?"

"This is not, of course, the purpose of our visit. But since you understand the matter, I need say no more. Señorita Isabella, I look forward with some considerable pleasure to Sunday." He came round the desk and she stood up, and he led the way to the office door. "And I hope the day will remain in our memories as – well, I say no more. Until Sunday morning then, when I return from Valldemosa to collect you – I must of course go this afternoon and stay there for a night or two at least – hasta la vista," and he kissed her hand with his usual care, and she went off to lunch feeling both touched and amused. That he had been anxious about her response to his invitation was obvious; clearly he wanted to please his elderly mother, and had feared for a moment that she would not accept the suggestion that the old lady should be given the chance to look over the nurse she had been instrumental in employing. Equally clearly, he took a certain perverse pride in her old fashioned ways, and in warning her of them, had really been boasting a little of his more than ordinary aristocratic antecedents. And it was that that amused her, in a gentle unmalicious way, amused her because hitherto, he had shown none of the warm ordinary human faults that other people had. To find that the remote, the formal and the all-too-perfect Sebastian Garcia had so broad a streak of old fashioned snobbery in his makeup was really rather fun.

She went into lunch full of pleasurable anticipation of the weekend's jaunt, and resolved not to let Sebastian feel at any time that she had let him down. She would impress this aristocratic old Spanish lady or her name wasn't Isabel Cameron!

She dressed with more than usual care on Sunday morning, rejecting two or three outfits as too flighty, or too revealing, or too sophisticated, settling in the end for a navy and white tailored dress of some severity. With white gloves and a neat white bag to complete her outfit, she looked, she told her reflection in the mirror, a perfectly suitable type to work in the hotel of an aristocrat – and then grimaced at herself and hurried down to meet Sebastian.

He was waiting for her in the foyer and greeted her with an air of portentousness that at first amused her a good deal; she was beginning to realize that Sebastian nursed not only respect for his old mother, but a definite awe. She remembered fleetingly the way Jaime Mendoza had talked of "the Señora" on the day she had arrived at the Cadiz, and for the first time felt a sharp twinge of anxiety. Was this visit perhaps more than a piece of kindness to an old lady (which was how she had seen her trip to Valldemosa up to now). Was it perhaps a confrontation with a formidable personality which could be embarrassing at best, or job-losing at worst?

She looked at Jaime, standing behind his desk in the posture of alert and very responsible managership he always wore when Sebastian was anywhere about, and he looked at her for a moment and then looked away, almost as though he were embarrassed, and her uneasiness grew. Clearly, Jaime saw some special significance in this visit; perhaps she might indeed come back to the Cadiz tonight with her marching orders.

"Do I look right, Sebastian?" she asked anxiously. "I tried to choose something that would be suitable – "

"Indeed, you look very suitable," he said, and smiled at her. "Sometimes a hat is considered necessary on formal occasions, but since this occasion, though of some significance, is not to be unduly formal, then a hat is not a matter of great importance. Mendoza! We return tonight. If there are any severe problems during the course of the day, you know of course where I can be reached. Now, Isabella, we depart – "

Jaime held the door open for them himself, hurrying round his desk to wave the hall porter away so that he

184

could perform the office, and as they went through he looked at Isabel with a gaze of such mournful intensity that she was again embarrassed. From the beginning she had seen him as a joke, pure and simple, and regarded his attempts to flatter her as so much nonsense; but looking at him today she thought perhaps he really had wanted to get to know her better, and was hurt because she accepted Sebastian's advances while rejecting his own.

"God help us!" she told herself, climbing into the passenger seat of the big car as Sebastian held the door open for her, "it would be all too easy to have my head turned here! All these people fussing over me – it's only because I look different to the local girls; that's all. They're being dazzled by carroty hair – "

Sebastian was driving himself today, and he handled the car with great skill, sweeping it round corners and along the broad boulevards, already filling with strollers early though it was, with smoothness and ease. He spoke little until they were out of the town and its suburbs, and moving across the flat plain towards the blue green mountains thrusting themselves craggily against the vivid blue sky.

And when he did start to talk, it was on a very superficial level, pointing out interesting sights they passed, from simple things like huge fig-laden cactus clumps or extraordinarily gnarled and ancient olive trees, to modern hotel blocks or pretty farmhouses. And her uneasiness grew, for she was now even more convinced that she was to be displayed to Señora Garcia, to have her suitability for her job assessed by the ultimate authority. Why else should Sebastian be so very neutral, so very correct and remote? Even for him, this morning's behaviour was noticeable for its restraint.

But as the drive went on, she began to relax. After all, what was the worst that could happen? As she'd told herself before during this summer on the island, all that anyone could do would be to fire her. If she were sent home, well, so what? She could return to her job at the Royal whenever she wanted, she knew that; Matron would welcome her with open arms, for well trained theatre sisters were hard to come by. And if going back to the Royal meant the misery of seeing Jay again, she'd have to put up with it. And anyway, she didn't have to go back to the Royal even if the old lady waiting for them up there in her mountain village did decide that she wanted to get rid of her enfermera. There were plenty of jobs, plenty of opportunities for a Royal trained nurse –

So she relaxed, and began to watch the scenery with the usual pleasure she found in the island's beauty, the greenish grey leaves of the olive trees, the pink and blue and yellow washed houses, the goats belled and tethered, the Don Quixote type windmills.

There had been a long silence between them as the big car swallowed the miles and the mountains marched nearer, filling more and more of the windscreen-framed view with their massy shapes. The flat fields had become fewer giving way to narrow terraces of earth on which olive and almond trees fought for ascendancy, when he said, "Look back."

Obediently, she turned her head, and then swivelled round even more, her breath catching with delight at what she saw. They had clearly been climbing steadily, for now the plain lay behind them, undulating with colour variations, and beyond it, in a soft haze of heat and smoke was Palma, edged by its silvery blue cloak of bay, and crowned with the cathedral. The building seemed to ride above the city in a bubble of air, its great spires and towers floating like silk banners, and she marvelled at the incredible skills and dreams and imaginings of the medieval craftsmen who had built it. To create such a

186

building today, with all the aids of modern science, would be achievement enough; that it had been built so many hundreds of years ago said almost more than could be comprehended of the quality of those men of the past.

Haltingly she tried to say some of this to Sebastian, and he turned his attention briefly from the road and smiled at her, that melting rare smile of his, and said "I'm happy. It is important to me that you should have this feeling for my ancestors. For they were among the builders of the cathedral and the city – of the entire island, in many ways. I am happy you understand. But, I knew of course, that you did. Why else this journey, hmm? Ah – see ahead there? Above those terraces? There is Valldemosa – my Valldemosa. To me, it looks not as though it were built, but as though it grew out of the rocks – "

The houses and churches and the great convent buildings climbed away up the side of the mountain, curling into the clefts of rock trustingly and so elegantly that she knew at once what he meant, and nodded her agreement, and he turned his head and smiled at her again, and she smiled back, feeling better than she had since leaving the hotel.

And then, they were there, sweeping along a great yellow dusty road edged with tall trees that was a cool airy avenue that finished in a small central plaza, and he eased the car in behind another much smaller one and switched off the engine before turning to her.

"So, I think perhaps we park the car here and look a little at the village before we go to my house. Madre does not expect us for perhaps another half an hour, so – we use the time to visit Valldemosa itself, yes?"

He helped her out of the car, and for a moment she shivered a little in the morning air, for bright and strong as the sunshine was, still there was a bit of ice in the air, and he smiled and took her elbow in that warm protective grip.

187

"You feel the breath of the mountains, yes? Even now, in the height of the summer it is always here cool, and chill, and comfortable. Below in the plains the heat can sit on your back like a grinning monkey, but up here, always peace and cool and comfort – "

They walked through the town, small and neat and pretty, and she looked about her with real pleasure. The houses with their tiled plaques depicting some favourite saint, carefully affixed beside each front door; the tiny shops tucked away behind small shuttered façades; the gardens of the convent, filled with the affectionate greenness of trees and shrubs; the broad paved courtyard of the convent itself with its well, its old ladies in shawls selling incredibly delicate crochet work and embroidery – it was all enchanting.

And finally, he took her to the inevitable bodega, to drink a glass of wine ("to take the mountain chill from your bones," he said, smiling down at her) and she was even more enchanted, for in the centre of the vast room they came into as they ducked under the low lintel of the doorway was an ancient well, with a huge bucket-bedecked wheel above it, and black beams and white walls and rough-hewn wooden tables and chairs.

"It's so absurdly story book!" she said, standing in the middle of the room and staring about her, at the vast barrels let into the walls, and cut away to provide shelves which were loaded with dusty green wine bottles. "I mean, there were pictures of places like this in my books when I was a child, but I never thought they really *existed*."

"Indeed, they do! This one is a little spoiled, perhaps – you see? The cheap souvenirs, the rubbish they sell – "

He pointed to tables laden with music boxes shaped like grand pianos, with dolls dressed in flamenco costumes, and toy bulls with miniature banderillas in their shoulders, and grimaced.

"Well, perhaps – they are rather ugly, I agree. But the room itself – nothing could spoil that."

"No. We drink, yes? You will leave it to me?"

"As long as it isn't too heady," she said. "It's not much after eleven in the morning after all, and there's still your mother to face – I mean, I'd not like to meet her in a state of incomplete control of myself!"

He laughed. "You need not fear. What I bring you is good – now, you see there in the corner? Go in there and sit and I come to you with our collation – "

In the corner was a classic Spanish fireplace, a small room with a hole in the ceiling beneath which burned, on a stone slab in the middle of the floor, a great log fire. Round the walls of the little room were settles with goatskins thrown over them, and she settled herself into one corner, breathing in the scent of wood smoke and trying to push down the uneasiness that was threatening to rise in her again.

He brought two glasses of amber wine, and a plate of sweet soft almond biscuits, and they raised their glasses at each other, and sipped, and she let the wine slide over her tongue and exclaimed her delight at the taste.

"It's – what does it taste of? It's awfully sweet, but it's like – oh, I don't know. Bottled sunshine?"

"That is an elegant way to describe it!" he said. "It is the local muscatel – the village is famous for it. The taste is of the grapes – like sipping flowers and fruit, is it not?"

The next half hour went by very swiftly as the wine warmed her to a rosy glow, and relaxed her so that incipient uneasiness quite melted away. And when he looked at his watch and said "Ah – it is near to noon, and we are expected, yes? I think we go now – " she stood up quite happily, and followed him from the bar with smiles and nods for the people who wished her a soft "Buenos diás!" as she passed them, and felt no nervousness at all.

But by the time they reached the car again and were driving along the narrow twisting streets of the village, the tension was returning, and she sat silently as he drove on, feeling the warmth of the wine shivering away to be replaced by nervousness.

The car swerved sharply, and she held on to the door as it slid into darkness and then out again into the cool green light of a paved courtyard. They had driven under an archway, and she peered out in fascination. The courtyard was not very big, but beautifully balanced, with the inevitable well in the middle, complete with winch and chain and bucket, and on each side the buildings rose to end in a steeply sloping roof under which a long balustraded gallery ran right round. The windows below the gallery were shuttered with green painted wooden slats, and everywhere there were plants, vines and bay trees and shrubs in pots.

The total effect was utterly delightful and when he had opened the door of the car for her and helped her out, she said impulsively, "But this is beautiful! How can you bear to be in Palma, even in such a modern and splendid hotel as the Cadiz, when you have a home like this?"

"Because I must earn my living, for myself and for my family," he said, and led the way across the uneven stones of the courtyard towards a door on the far side. "To have such a home is, I agree, a delightful matter – but people must eat, and I as the man of this household must be responsible for this. The days when our land could maintain us are long gone, Isabella. But I do not distress myself too much. My mother lives here, and I can come to refresh myself from time to time.

"And I can think of the day when I bring here, for always another lady to care for the house and the people of it. Yes?"

"Yes," she said, and could think of nothing more to

say. For they had gone through the door he was holding open, and were standing in a wide room with a richly tiled floor gleaming with age and polish, and walls on which the most splendid of Persian carpets hung, with heavy, almost black, carved wood furniture, and white walls to set off the whole. The total effect was a restrained richness, of years of cultured taste culminating in the creation of the perfect setting for a life of peace and scholarliness and art.

"You like it?" he said softly, and she could only nod and stare, but he seemed contented with her reaction, and led her further into the house. They went into two other rooms, one a dining room, rich with brass ornaments and showing its Moorish influences strongly in the fretted metal of the low hanging lamps and the low couches about the walls; the other a more relaxed and comfortable but still very rich sitting room.

"And now, I take you to the sitting room of my mother. She awaits us there, as always – "

He led her back, through the rooms they had already seen, and across the courtyard to a door on the far side, and this time it was opened for them by a middle-aged woman in a heavy black dress, her hair pulled back severely from her face.

"Buenos diás, Señor," she said and her voice was soft and pleasant to listen to. Sebastian nodded at her, and spoke in crisp Spanish, and she answered in the same soft tones, and then he turned to Isabel, taking her elbow to lead her through the door the woman was holding invitingly open.

"My mother is well, and waiting for us. I saw her last night, of course – but I left for Palma this morning too early to disturb her. But she is anxious to see us. Come."

Through a narrow passage way, across a small inner hall, through another door, and into a room so cluttered, so filled with furniture and pictures and plants and rugs that it made Isabel feel breathless, as though the weight of years was pressing on her shoulders. She saw with one swift comprehensive glance that this was because of what the room contained, for the pictures, the photographs of men on horseback, women in stiff studio poses, children in communion dresses, eyes soulfully uplifted above the folded hands, clearly spanned the past half century. The ornaments that crammed the crowded little tables, the cushions and embroidered covers – all reminded her powerfully of her own grandmother's room, the one in which she had spent the last bedridden years of her life, with all her memories clutched round her like a blanket.

Across the room was a window, open and unshuttered, and looking out onto a pretty walled garden which was a riot of greenery and colour. And sitting in front of the window in a high backed chair, her feet on a footstool and her legs wrapped in a rug was the most wrinkled woman Isabel could ever remember seeing.

Her hair was as black as Sebastian's own, and strained back from her forehead so tightly that it seemed to be pulling out at the roots at the line where it met her forehead. Beneath it, her eyes were dark and very bright, but all round them, the skin that was as sallow and olive in tone as Sebastian's was creased and twisted into a myriad lines, so that for one irreverent moment, Isabel found herself thinking of her as a very old and gnarled walnut –

Sebastian had left her standing at the door to move immediately over to the old lady and kiss her on both cheeks, and murmur to her, and then, even as Isabel started to feel uncomfortable posed there in the doorway, he turned and beckoned to her, while still speaking softly to the old lady. She nodded, and stared very directly at Isabel, listening but keeping her mouth firmly closed.

Isabel moved forwards, a little awkwardly, as Sebastian broke into English.

"Isabella, I present you to my mother, who bids me welcome you to her home and thanks you for your company."

The old lady jerked her chin slightly, indicating a chair, and Sebastian stepped forwards and pulled the chair out a little, so that Isabel could sit down, and said, "My mother asks that you make yourself comfortable, and wishes to know whether you will take a little wine, or perhaps coffee with her?"

Looking at the old lady, sitting there staring at her unblinkingly with her lips still tightly closed, Isabel wondered wildly for a moment whether she was communicating with her son by telepathy, and then almost giggled aloud, for the whole thing was becoming more and more story book, as Sebastian added, in exactly the same tone of voice, "I would suggest you say you would like coffee, Isabella, for this would be proper."

"Then indeed, I'll take some coffee, if I must," she said, and tentatively smiled at the old lady, who merely sat and looked back at her.

Sebastian spoke to her again, and this time she nodded briefly, and he picked up a small bell from the table beside the old lady's chair and rang it, and so quickly that it was obvious she had been standing outside the door waiting for it, the housekeeper in her black dress came in, bearing a tray in her hands.

The next ten minutes were filled with the ritual of coffee pouring, of offers of milk and sugar, biscuits and cake, and then the housekeeper was gone, and the three of them were sitting solemnly staring at each other and sipping from the very delicate china cups the thick black brew they had been given.

And then started what was for Isabel the most extra-ordinary half hour she had ever spent in her life. The old lady started to question in a cracked rather deep voice, never taking her eyes from Isabel's face, and showing no response of any sort to the answers Isabel gave and which Sebastian again translated.

The incredible thing was the questions the old lady pro-duced; questions of so breathtakingly personal a nature, probing into her family's history, their occupations, her father's income, her own reasons for following the career she had, the amount of money she had earned, how she had spent it, what she had saved, questions about her religious and political beliefs, her health, wanting to know of her childhood illnesses, the life she had led in Scotland as compared with London, the social life she had chosen, the number of men she had known, her attitudes towards them – it went on and on.

But what was most incredible of all to Isabel was the way that she answered this catechism. She would never cease to wonder at that: the way that she had seemed to accept as normal this old lady's outrageous probing, her positively impertinent questioning and had answered in almost total honesty, only balking at the queries about her men friends. She said calmly, "That I can't remember," when Sebastian translated the query and repeated the same answer to all similar questions.

But she felt no sense of personal outrage or offence about it. In the setting of that cluttered yet elegant room, with the garden and its colour and scents beyond the window, with Sebastian sitting there between them, it all seemed utterly natural and right.

And then, at last, the questions stopped, and the old lady sat as still as ever, looking at Isabel with that same beady black stare, and then, sharply, nodded, and held out one wrinkled old claw of a hand.

Instinctively, Isabel stood up and glanced at Sebastian, who nodded approvingly. So she stepped forwards to take the hand in her own, feeling the papery skin, dry and delicate, against her own warm and rather damp palm.

The old lady leaned forwards very slightly, and spoke in the same throaty voice, and Isabel looked questioningly at Sebastian who smiled and said only, "I will tell you of this remark later – for now, Isabella, I ask you simply to say your goodbyes, and wait for me in the courtyard, for I must speak with my mother for a few moments before we leave. You permit?"

"Of course – " she said, and nodded and smiled at the old lady, and let go her hand, and then, almost feeling she should have left the room backwards, she picked up her gloves and bag and went out, closing the door behind her very softly.

Almost at once the housekeeper was there in the cool shadowy hallway, and led her through the way they had come back to the courtyard, and then bobbing her head slightly went away, leaving her to take deep breaths of the iced mountain air and blink up at the square of sunlit sky high above, before almost collapsing onto the coping of the well to recover herself.

16

He came out ten minutes later, and stood there at the doorway of the house, looking at her with his head poised a little to one side, and she looked back at him, a little anxiously and with a questioning look on her face.

"Well? Am I to be fired on the spot? Or will the Señora permit me to remain at the Cadiz to complete the season?" she asked in as light a voice as she could conjure up.

He smiled at her indulgently, as one would at a sweet but silly child, and came across the courtyard to sit beside her on the narrow coping of the well.

"You make a joke, yes, Isabella? Although perhaps, it is not so funny. For indeed it may be considered by Madre, when later we discuss more detailed plans, that it is not quite proper for you to remain at the Cadiz as enfermera – "

She stared at him, her face creased with puzzlement. "What? Not *proper*? How do you mean, not proper? Are you trying to tell me that she doesn't like me? That she *does* think I ought to leave the Cadiz? Because if that's the case, I'll tell you this much – "

He raised his hands, and took her face between them, looking down at her with his eyes narrowed into a smile, and then, cutting off the spate of words that had risen in her, he bent his head and kissed her with a calm possessiveness that took her breath away far more than did the kiss itself, totally unexpected though it was.

For a few seconds she sat there, stunned with surprise, and then, she pulled back and pushed him away, and said breathlessly, "And what the hell do you imagine you're doing? Of all the daft, crazy – what are you about, man? Are you quite daft? I asked you whether – what – ah, will you *explain*?"

"But it is obvious, is it not? You are a woman of intelligence as well as spirit and charm, my Isabella. You knew why we came here this morning, just as you know now what I mean, what it is – *aboot*," and he smiled at his own very bad imitation of her accent.

"I don't know what you're talking about!" Isabel said furiously. "And if you don't *immediately* explain, I'll – "

"So! You wish of course to have me say all as it should be said. This is of course right. From the start we have been always careful to behave as we should. So, Señorita Isabella – my beautiful Isabella, I ask you to become my wife. In a few days, I will arrange for you to talk with my lawyers, since you have, sadly, no relations who can serve this purpose for you, and then, we arrange for our wedding at the end of the summer – "

His voice trailed away, and for a long moment they sat there on the edge of the well, staring at each other, and she knew her face was filled with an expression of horror, knew it was there as surely as she knew the look of stunned surprise was on his. And then he said sharply, "Why do you look at me like this, Isabella? You knew, surely, you knew what it was I was to say – you cannot look at me like that, as though you are surprised! It is another of your Scottish jokes, yes? It is not that you do not understand – "

"Sebastian, for God's sake! Are you – why should you think any such thing? Of course I'm surprised – I'm – I've never had a shock like it in my life! Why should you think that I ever meant – that I should

197

ever think that you – oh – this is absolutely crazy. Mad! – "

"But we – I explained! I said to you, I *explained*! When I arranged to bring you here to see my mother, when I told you how she is, that she is a lady of the old days that with her all is always very formal, very proper, you agreed to come! Had you not wished to accept my proposal you should have said then, should have said you would prefer not to disturb my mother, and then, for both of us, no pain, no embarrassment, nor difficulty! I believed we understood each other!"

He stood up, and began to move about the courtyard, pacing heavily and angrily from one side to the other, his back rigid with anger.

"And at the restaurant, when you spoke to me of the situation with Squires! For what other reason, Señorita? For what possible reason does a woman tell a man of such a matter unless she intends to inform him that he has the chance for which he had been waiting? I do not comprehend your behaviour, Señorita, unless you are giving me again the joke of your country that I do not understand."

"Sebastian, my God, I'm sorry – I had no idea – when you asked me why I was fed up and were so friendly and kind. I thought – but why should you think I was inviting any such thing as – ah, come on, Sebastian! It's *you* that's joking, surely?"

She sat there, still and rigid on the narrow wall, her hands gripping her bag, and staring at him, filled with a disbelieving shame; not again, not twice in so short a space of time! What was the matter with this island? Was there something in the air, some mad effect of the blazing sun that made such things happen? To have left an almost shattered heart in London, because the one man she had ever cared for had rejected her, only to have two other men fall at her feet within a matter of weeks – it was sheer lunacy. And she essayed a smile, tried to laugh, to show him she knew it was all ludicrous, absurd.

But he was standing very still and staring at her, his face tight and angry and then he said in a choked and very quiet voice, "You told me that you had rejected the advances of the man Squires because of your love for another man. You sat in the restaurant and you looked at me and said you could not accept Squires for this reason, and on your face is a look of such affection, such – such desire, that for the first time since I met you and knew you were the one for whom I am waiting so long, I am sure. The weeks of patience and friendship have led to the love I am hoping for, and then, when I tell you of the visit to my mother, and you accept I think, yes! My Isabella loves me, she wishes for me, and when I have shown her to the Madre, then, all is clear for us – "

"Sebastian, you've misunderstood, totally, and horribly, and – oh God I wish I'd never said a damned word! Look, when I said I loved someone else it wasn't *you* I meant. What sort of woman would I be to do such a thing? You of all people with all your fuss about the right way to go about things – you should *know* no decent girl is going to tell a man she loves him when – when – Ye Gods, Sebastian, I'm no' denying there were a few times when I thought you were damned attractive – you are, *very* attractive – but as for loving – no, of course not! Heaven help me, I came here to get over the man I do love and who – and now Biff *and* you – oh, it's too much!"

And she jumped to her feet, scrabbling her gloves and bag into her shaking hands and fled, stopping only for one brief second to look back over her shoulder at him standing there, ludicrously framed in vine leaves and palms.

And then she was running full tilt along the dusty road

back towards the village, anywhere to escape from his stillness and hurt pride.

He caught up with her halfway up the long road, pulling the car in beside her and leaning over to open the door.

"Get in," he said curtly. "There is no way to Palma except the return with me. And it is hot and you are already disturbed by your haste."

She hesitated, standing there on the hot dusty road, feeling the cool mountain air on her flaming damp cheeks, gasping a little from the rush of her flight, and knew she was being absurd, and after a moment more of hesitation, got into the car to sit rigidly beside him, her face red with a sick combination of shame and exertion, while he sat grim and tight beside her, driving the car as hard and fast as it would go.

They were almost out of the mountains and into the plains before she spoke again, and then she said in a tight but very controlled voice, "There is something I must ask you."

"By all means," and his voice was even more controlled and colourless than her own.

"Let us suppose, for one moment, that I did – that I would have been prepared to accept your very – kind proposal of marriage. Would you, under any circumstances, have made such a proposal without first consulting your mother, introducing me?"

He frowned, and turned and looked at her for a fleeting moment before returning his attention to his driving.

"Before? – No, of course not. This is not the way of my family, nor will it ever be. We are people of breeding and good behaviour, a fact which I had believed you understood. We are not the gypsies, the people of the roads with no roots, no traditions! We are Garcia of Valldemosa, and as such we behave by the rules. Always."

"And suppose that your mother had not agreed that I

was a suitable wife for you? I gather she *did* in fact agree to accept me?"

"She had some misgivings about the free life you have led in England, but accepted that this reflected no direct fault in you, but was part of the lax attitudes towards such matters in that country. Your willingness – as we understood it – to accept the forms of behaviour of ourselves we both saw as an assurance that your life in London had not unduly damaged your moral character."

"My moral – Señor Garcia, even accepting that different people have very different attitudes and ideas, I find that a piece of outrageous arrogance! My moral character! How *dare* you tell me that your mother sat there making judgements on my morals! It's a piece of the most – "

"Since this matter has come to an end in the manner it has, I see no reason why we should descend to further recrimination, Señorita," and his voice crackled as icily as the mountain tops they were now leaving behind them.

She took a deep breath and after a moment nodded her head crisply.

"All right. But let me ask you again. Suppose that she had *not* accepted me as suitable. That she had said 'No, she is not fit to be your wife'. What would you have done then?"

He shrugged. "Done? What do you expect I would have done?"

"Have told her where to get off, that's what!"

"I do not understand."

"Told her that you're a man in your own right, and that you'd choose your wife as and where you wanted, and to the devil with her and her opinions! That's what I'd expect a *real* man to say."

She knew her voice was rising with anger, but didn't care a whit, and went on recklessly. "I'd no' expect any

201

grown man in a position like yours to knuckle down to the bullying of an old woman who – "

"It seems to me, Señorita, that in the misunderstanding that we have suffered, both of us have been fortunate," he said and his voice was as colourless and calm as ever, underlining her own heatedness. "For, as a gentleman of Spain, I must assure you that the woman who will come first in my life always is my mother. However important to a man his wife may be, as his partner and as the mother of his children, the mother is of prime importance, always. If you had not been able to accept that, then never could we have made any sort of happiness together. It seems to me that I have been more fortunate than I realized a little while ago. My pride was damaged, I do not deny, for no man of my breeding is accustomed to rejection from any such source. But this I will recover from far sooner than I would have recovered, I suspect, from the damage that would have ensued from a marriage between us."

He drove on, composed and apparently relaxed, and she could have shaken him, could have reached out and hit him in her irritation at the calm arrogance of him, at the ease with which he apparently had been able to accept her refusal of him, coming as it did so soon after that insulting questioning meeting with the Señora Garcia. It was almost more than she could stand.

But then, as the car purred on its way into Palma, and the narrow poverty stricken streets of the outskirts became wider, changed their character into the richer shoplined boulevards of the town centre, she relaxed. After all, at least she didn't have to feel guilty about this man, as she did about Biff, which was some small comfort –

And then she remembered, realized how with both Biff and this cold arrogant creature sitting beside her, it had been her own stupidity that had caused them to react as they did, and her face flamed with mortification. What sort of girl was she to treat men so? What had happened to her? It would be a long time before she would be able to live with the memory of her own behaviour, she told herself drearily as they stopped outside the Cadiz, and he came round the car, with chilly punctiliousness, to open the door for her.

She stood there on the pavement for a while, staring up at the hotel, and then at him, and suddenly bit her lip and looked away.

"It's going to be very difficult to go on here after this, isn't it?" she said and didn't know what she wanted him to answer. To stay or go? Which should she do? And which would he want her to do?

He moved across the pavement towards the entrance, carefully and formally indicating the way. And said quite quietly with no expression at all on his face. "It is to me a matter of supreme unimportance, Señorita. Should you stay, I need not see you any more than I need see any member of my staff in whom I am not particularly interested. You can deal with Mendoza. Should you decide to go, then it is equally unimportant for I can obtain a replacement for you very easily."

The hall porter had seen them, and was holding the door open invitingly, and he looked back over his shoulder before walking quickly in towards his mirror-doored office.

"Very easily indeed," he repeated, and then he was gone, leaving her standing alone in the lobby.

17

To stay or to go? To sit it out, grimly, to the end of the season, or scamper for home, tail between legs, away from the sidelong glances and ill-hidden sniggers that would be inevitable once the Cadiz staff realized that Sebastian was no longer taking her out? The question slid in and out of her consciousness, came between her and work, reared up and shrieked at her from her mirror when she brushed her hair, came up at her from her plate as she ate –

For three days she went on in this state of indecision, at one moment determined to go straight up to her room and pack to catch the first plane home, the next finding all her Scottish stubbornness building up to make her set her mouth and harden her resolve; damned if she'd let any tuppenny ha'penny Spanish hotel owner make *her* do anything she didn't fully want to do! – and then once more depression and shame would overcome her, and again she'd decide to pack.

And then, on the fourth morning, as she was completing the clinic and dealing with the last patient, a man from the gardening staff with an infected rose-thorn wound in his hand, she heard someone come into the surgery room, and looked over her shoulder, irritated, for patients were supposed to wait outside until called for. But even as the words of reproof rose to her lips, she closed her mouth again, for Vanda Connaught was standing there, leaning against the door jamb with all her usual arrogance.

"You wanted something?" Isabel said shortly, turning back to the gardener and continuing with the bandaging of his hand.

"It's a personal matter," Vanda said and it seemed to Isabel that her insolent drawl was even more than usually exaggerated, and she bit her lip to force back her irritation, and said nothing.

"Le dille aqui? Does it hurt here?" she asked the man, touching his hand again and he shook his head and grinned, and she smiled at him. "Pasado mañana – la venda fresca – "

"The day after tomorrow – a fresh bandage?" the man said, proud of his few words of English, and went away happily nodding nervously at Vanda Connaught as he squeezed past her at the door, she not moving an inch to allow him to pass.

"Well?" Isabel said frostily, as she began to clear away the dressing tray and scrub the instruments. It was easier to talk to this woman while her hands were busy, when she didn't have to look at her directly. "You want me on a personal matter? Personal to me or to you?"

"Both," Vanda Connaught said. "In a way," and laughed softly and Isabel threw a startled glance at her. She had never heard Vanda Connaught sound so relaxed, so happy.

"I don't see how that could be," she said. "We've hardly that much in common, have we?"

Vanda Connaught laughed again, and moved across the surgery to perch herself on the operating table, watching Isabel's deft fingers as she completed her tidying up operations. "You'd be surprised how much we have in common, Miss Nursie," she said. "Or maybe you wouldn't. Anyway – tell me. Is it true? That you and Sebastian have had a row?"

"A row? I don't have rows with people."

205

"Hey, pitchy putchy! Don't we sound dignified! Too good to be true, aren't you?"

"Look, if you've come down here just to be disagreeable, Mrs. Connaught, I'm not in any mood for it, so will you just turn about and leave me in peace! Go on – away with you! I'm no' going to be badgered by – "

"Oh, I'm sorry! I'm sorry! I didn't mean to upset you! Now, for heaven's sake, take no notice of the way I talk – I've a sharp tongue but it doesn't mean much – and *talk* to me, will you? I really want to know – "

Isabel blinked, and felt the angry colour that had risen in her cheeks begin to subside as she stared at the other woman, puzzlement filling her.

"Oh, don't look at me like that! I'm nothing like as nasty an individual as I might seem sometimes! I treated you rather badly, didn't I? At first? I suppose you've a right to be a bit off. But look – I'm sorry! I was rude and nasty to you, and I admit it, and I'm *sorry*! Will you accept that?"

Isabel moved then, and came to perch beside the other woman on the operating table. "I can hardly do otherwise, can I. But you'll forgive me if I'm a shade suspicious! I mean, after all this time to suddenly – I can't help wondering what it is you're after – "

"Canny – canny!" Vanda said, and grinned a little crookedly at her. "You remind me a bit of my – my late husband. He was of Scots extraction as they say – " she shrugged sharply. "Ancient history. Okay, call it an armed truce. But answer my question, will you? *Have* you and Sebastian had a r – er – *disagreement*?"

Now it was Isabel's turn to produce a crooked smile. "You could call it that, I suppose. Anyway, there's no' much point in denying that we're not precisely on speaking terms, is there? He ignores me totally when he sees me, and I ignore him, and we don't ever get together now."

"Please, what happened?" Vanda leaned forwards and touched Isabel's hand, making her look up, and her face was filled with a most curious expression, half pleading, half avid. "I've a reason for asking."

"It'll have to be a damned good reason to make me talk that easily about my private affairs!" Isabel said spiritedly. "I'm not one of your let's-let-our-back-hair-down types, nor ever have been."

"Oh, damn you!" Vanda slid to her feet and began to prowl edgily about the surgery but there was no rancour in her voice. "Damn you for being so – so – oh, for God's sake, girl! Can't you tell why for yourself? As far as I'm concerned the sun shines out of that man's ears, and always has. For years – more years than I care to remember, he's protected me, looked after me, taken care of my pride as well as my financial needs, when he didn't have to – "

"What did you say?" Isabel said softly.

"What? That he's taken care of my pride, you mean?" Vanda said. "Oh, it's a long tale. But years ago, he and my husband were partners. My husband treated him like – he did a lot of stupid things, shall we say. And Sebastian bought him out – and then when my stupid idiot of a husband went and killed himself, Sebastian took me on, pretended I was his partner – "

"You *know*?" Isabel said, staring at her. "You know? You've always known?"

"Oh, of course I have! Did he tell you about it? Ye Gods, you must have got under his skin. He's never told a soul – if he had you can be bloody sure I'd know. He told you – " Her face suddenly hardened, losing the gentler softness that had seemed to be there for the past few minutes. "Then maybe there's no point in my being here. If he told you that."

"It was after – after that – uh – disagreement we had,

207

you and I. I think he was trying to explain a little of why – " Isabel said, embarrassment wrapping her in a hot blanket.

"Huh! Yeah, well – I suppose. Anyway, I might as well tell you the rest, even if I'm past – so! The sun shines out of his ears. I – " she stopped her prowling and turned to stare at Isabel, and now her face looked naked, and so filled with appeal that for a moment Isabel felt her eyes prickle with tears.

"I love him, you see. And I don't know what to do about it. He's kind to me, polite to me, protective – but I could be his bloody maiden aunt for all there is of anything else. And when I saw the way he looked at you, the very first day you got here, watched him fancying you, I wanted to – well, anyway, I was angry. Which is why I – But now – please tell me. What's happening now? Is it all over? Or just a temporary thing? I suppose it is. If he told you such private things – "

"It's over," Isabel said after a long pause. "It's very much over. He'll never speak to me again, nor I to him. That's for certain. I can promise you that."

Vanda looked at her for a long time, her eyes searching her face, and then, very slowly, in a great wave.

"Then – Thank you. Really, thank you. I've no pride left, you see. I'm past caring what you or anyone else thinks of me. I love him, and I'll do anything I can to get him. One of these days, surely, one of these days – "

Isabel stood up suddenly. "Come into the office," she said crisply. "I've some of the makings of a cup of coffee – "

Vanda laughed then. "I thought you weren't one of the let-your-back-hair-down type?" she said jeeringly. "And here we go, hauling out the coffee cups!"

"I'm not. I'm a nurse, though, and I know what to do when people have problems. But if you don't want help

208

– or the coffee – then you go and take a running jump at yourself!" Isabel said sharply.

"Okay. Okay! Later on, I'll take a running jump. Right now, I take my coffee black, no sugar."

She made the coffee with hot water drawn from the water sterilizer, and they sat in silence for a while sipping, and then Isabel said carefully "You want Garcia. You want to marry him, is that it?"

"Yes," Vanda said it badly, making no attempt to hide her feelings, and Isabel grinned at her.

"If you'd shown your virtues as clearly as you showed your nastiness, right there at the beginning, we could have been friends, you know that, Vanda? I like honest people – "

"So stop being so po-faced and stop lecturing me. Just tell me what it is you've dreamed up to solve my problem, in that clever nurse's head of yours," Vanda jeered, but she smiled as she said it.

"He's a – peculiar man," Isabel said carefully. "Curious, I mean. He lives here in one of the most cosmopolitan towns in the world, he's rich, he runs a highly successful business, yet he's managed to pretend to himself that he's still living back in the eighteenth century. It's a most extraordinary thing – "

"Hell, I know that! Go teach your grandmother to suck eggs!"

"Well, if you know it, then you're stupid to behave with him the way you do, without stopping to think about the way he thinks a woman ought to be!"

"How do you mean? I can't change the way I look, if that's what you're saying! If he's got a fancy for carroty hair and green eyes, what do I do? Dye it? that'll help a lot, I don't think!"

"Ah, no, woman! Where's your sense!" Isabel snapped. "It's got nothing to do with looks – or only marginally.

It's just that he wants a woman who behaves properly. His idea of properly. He thought I was one of his – one of those comme il faut types, who never do anything that isn't precisely proper and feminine and all the rest of it. It's all of a piece, of course. He saw in me what he wanted to see, never stopping to think that maybe I wasn't one of the retiring well behaved sit-at-home types he really admires. Anyway – you're not going to get far by getting drunk, nasty drunk at that, and making a great guy of yourself! So there you have it!"

Vanda sat staring sombrely into her cup. "I only do it because I'm depressed, and frustrated and lonely – "

"Hell, I know that. I know you aren't an alcoholic – yet. Though you will be if you go on the way you've been. You'll get nowhere with the great Garcia by being half smashed when you're with him. You might get somewhere by being quiet and civilized and – and clever."

"How clever?"

"You know his mother?"

"I've met the old trout, once or twice. Yes."

"Well, that's where he's vulnerable. Right there. If you want him, and you're prepared to get him on any terms – use his mother. If she told him to marry you, with his daft eighteenth century ideas I really believe he would. He mightn't love you at first, mightn't ever love you. But he feels responsible for you and that's a fair beginning. Feels guilty about you too. Show him you can change and be meek and proper, tell him the change was made by *him*, and who can say what'll happen? It's up to you to decide whether or not those are the terms you want him on, but if you do – " she shrugged. "Then it's his mother you want to work on. Not him. And keep away from the bottle, for heaven's sake!"

Vanda was staring at her, her eyes a little narrowed and

very bright. And then she smiled again, that slow smile that made her face look so much younger.

"I think you're right – I really think you're right. I'll visit her. Take my knitting and sit and talk to her, do the dutiful would-be-daughter-in-law bit – " she laughed, a sharp bark of laughter, and stood up and stretched her catlike languorous stretch, and smiled down at Isabel. "Thank you, Nursie! I'll say this for you – you're no dog in the manger, are you? You're right. We should have been friends."

"Bit late now," Isabel said shortly, and then held out her hand, impulsively. "Good luck, Vanda, I think it'll work – and any way it's worth trying, and it'll give you plenty to think about – "

After a moment, Vanda shook hands with her, and then said curiously, "What about you though? Are you at all – upset by this disagreement, whatever it was? I still don't know, do I?"

"Nor will you, not from me," Isabel said, and then shrugged. "Me? I'm not upset. Not in any basic way, certainly."

"Someone else? The Yank?"

"Yank? Oh, Biff – oh no! He – he was a very good friend. That's all."

"You've been piling up the past tenses, haven't you? Both your fellas, out in the cold?"

"Vanda, I have work to do, d'you mind? I'd like to get on with it – "

"Ah, stuff!" Vanda said, and shoved at her a little roughly, so that she had to sit down again. "Now it's my turn. You sat there and told me what to do, a flibberty bit like you, half my age, God damn you, and now it's my turn. So, what's *your* problem, Nursie?"

Isabel sat there, looking at the other woman's face with its lines of years of living etched on it and felt it rise in her, a great wave of loneliness, a desperate need to talk to someone, to pour it all out in words, and almost surprised to hear her own voice she said, "Someone at home. In London. I came here to get over him, and I can't. It's pretty bloody, one way and another."

Vanda nodded. "I imagine I know how you feel," she said dryly. "So why do you have to get over him? Did he chuck you?"

Isabel shrugged. "For the stupidest reasons. Said he wasn't good enough for me, on account he wasn't the marrying type – and that was what I wanted. So he put an end to it."

"Not an excuse? Not a quick way out because he fancied someone else ?" Vanda said baldly and Isabel winced slightly. "Yes, I know, I'm crude and coarse. But I know the way the world wags. So, was he alibi-ing out, or was it for real – I mean were you nagging him to marry you?"

"I was not!" Isabel said indignantly. "Indeed, I was not. I never mentioned the word, never asked him to – told him I loved him and that was all that mattered – and as for wanting out – he loves me too. Misses me like hell. I know that – " and her hand moved, touched the pocket of her uniform, where Jay's letter sat, as it always did. She had told herself she carried it on her in case one of the inquisitive chamber maids took to peering among the things in her room, but she knew that was an alibi of her own, knew that it was just that she couldn't bear not to keep it with her.

Vanda's eyes followed the gesture, and she said quickly, "You've had a letter from him since you got here? Then I guess maybe he does – show me."

"I will not!" Isabel said hotly. "Don't be so damned inquisitive!"

"Oh, stuff. Don't be so damned full of yourself! You

had the pleasure of telling me what to do, and now it's my turn. So show me, you daft wee thing!"

Almost against her will Isabel smiled at her imitation of her accent, and then, with an almost luxuriant sense of relief she took the letter from her pocket, and handed it over. And then sat, staring at her fingers interlocked on her lap as Vanda read it, listened to her breathing and the rustle of the paper as she turned the pages.

"You – you are so stupid!" Vanda said at length, but her voice sounded warm and friendly. "There's not a girl in the world who wouldn't give her eyeteeth to get a letter like that from a man she loves, and what do *you* do? Sit here moping instead of rushing home to him. Stupid, absolutely solid ivory from ear to ear!"

Isabel looked up at her, her face creased a little. "Stupid? But he says – "

"He says he loves you. The man's near demented for want of you – what more do you want? Sure, he's fighting tooth and nail not to have to admit it, not fully, but that's not so unusual. Men often do – but love you? Of course he does, and probably always will. Take my tip, ducky. Write him a letter, tell him you're coming home, and when you get there, you put your arms round him, and tell him you love him, and tell him he loves you – even though he knows it – and tell him that whether he likes it or not, you two are going to be married. He'll fight and he'll argue – damn it, you may even have to take him to buy you the ring! but he'll go along with you, and he'll be there on the day you set, I promise you. And then, once you're married, you'll see – he'll turn into the most satisfactory of suburban husbands ever, all wrapped up in mortgages and school bills and the rates. You'll see – "

"I – ah, you're crazy – how can you – "

"How can I be so sure? How can *you* be so sure that

you gave *me* the right advice? Do you think what you suggested will work for me?"

"Yes – yes, I do – "

"Then this is what's right for you. I'm as certain as you are. So do as you're told at once, will you? Go write the letter, book the next plane home, and he'll be there on the ground waiting for you. You'll see."

She moved away then, across the surgery to the door, and stopped for a moment and looked back over her shoulder. "Tell you what, nursie. Bring him here for your honeymoon. Here, to the Cadiz. By then, I'll be running the place with my – with Sebastian. It'll work for me, it's got to – and it'll work for you. So – " and now she grinned that crooked grin again. "Hasta la vista!"

EPILOGUE

The plane banked steeply, so that the wing rose high on one side to cut the sky with a sharp silvery line, and the fear that had thickened her throat when they took off but which had momentarily settled came bubbling up again. She turned her head to look out of the window beside her but that was worse, for there below her – so very far below! – was a lurching patchwork of brownish green fields, the cluster of glass-gleaming black and red roofed buildings that was Palma airport, the crawling ants of cars on the grey ribbons of road and this time she closed her eyes, and let her hands convulsively grip the buckle of her safety belt.

"Been on 'oliday then?" a voice said in her ear. "You've got a real lovely tan there, so it's a proper silly question, 'n it? I 'ave too. Smashin' place, Majorca, I reckon, don't you?"

She turned her head, and looked at him. A tall young man with a wide smile, rather long hair over an open-necked shirt, very white teeth in a sunbrowned face. He looked friendly, kind and relaxed, and she stared at him consideringly for a long moment before she opened her mouth to speak.

"No entiendo el inglés," she said loudly and clearly. "Soy española – " and the young man looked puzzled for a moment, and then nonplussed and then rather bored, and he nodded at her in a vague way before turning his head to look at the girl sitting on the other side of the gangway.

She leaned back in her seat, and unbuckled her safety belt, and relaxed. Just a couple of hours, and then Gatwick – and the road to London and the Royal –

She closed her eyes, happily snuggling back against the upholstery of the seat, and imagined it, how it would be, Jason standing there on the other side of the customs barrier, his hands in his trouser pockets, watching for her, and the way his eyebrows would go up and his mouth would crease into its familiar grin when he saw her and then his arms about her.

She grinned to herself, and let her mind slide away to Vanda, wondering how it was with her. They had met that morning as Isabel's luggage was being carried out of the Cadiz, under the fussy direction of Jaime Mendoza, and Isabel had laughed aloud at the sight of her, for she was wearing a very simple linen dress and a wide brimmed straw hat, and a bare minimum of makeup on her face.

"You're going to Valldemosa!" Isabel had said, and Vanda had smiled at her, her eyebrows raised quizzically, and said "Where else? I have a lunch date with an old lady – and what's with you? It worked?"

And Isabel had stepped forwards, and put her hands on the older woman's shoulders and kissed her cheek.

"I wrote, as you said. And he phoned me. Fifteen minutes it lasted for, it must have cost him a wee fortune! He'll be at Gatwick, he said. Thank you, Vanda. I'm as daft as you said, not recognizing what it was he was saying in that letter. He told me, though, in much better words, just what he meant – " She hugged the other's shoulders briefly, and then embarrassed, let go. "Thank you, and – all the best."

"I'll need it," Vanda had said with that sharply sour grin of hers, and then she was gone, hipping her way out of the hotel to the hired car that was waiting outside, and she had leaned out of the window and waved at Isabel.

And Isabel had waved back, and called, "Good luck – make it happen – do you hear? Make it happen – " and Vanda had grinned and nodded.

"In ten minutes we will be landing at Gatwick airport," the tinny voice of the intercom woke her. "Kindly fasten your safety belts – extinguish cigarettes – captain and crew hope you have enjoyed the flight – "

The music began to swell as the passengers rustled and hissed a little, and she turned her head to stare out of the port-hole at the ground below. Grey and greenish brown, there was the Surrey countryside, and somewhere inside that glass and chrome building was Jay.

Jay, and tomorrow, the rest of her life. She fastened her safety belt, and smiled happily to herself. She wasn't a bit frightened this time.